Love's Soft Whisper

JUNE MASTERS BACHER

HARVEST HOUSE PUBLISHERS
Eugene, Oregon 97402

Scripture quotations are taken from the King James Version of the Bible.

LOVE'S SOFT WHISPER

Eugene, Oregon 97402

ISBN 0-89081-559-3

Printed in the United States of America.

To
Truett and Norma,
Wrayanne,
Julie,
and Melissa

CONTENTS

Love's Soft Whisper

Ye are our epistle written in our hearts. . . written not with ink, but with the Spirit of the living God, not in tables of stone, but in fleshy tables of the heart.

—2 Corinthians 3:2,3

Human things must be known in order to be loved, but divine things must be loved in order to be known.

—Pascal

CHAPTER 1
To a World Unknown

Stunned, Courtney listened as her mother sent Maj, the Swedish maid, away. Mrs. Glamora would ring for the girl "when it is time to help Miss Courtney pack."

In just seconds the world had split in half. The two hemispheres were sucked into unexplored space, and Courtney was aboard neither of them. Instead, she floated weightlessly, lacking the power to bring herself into orbit. *Mother is sending me away again—and this time FAR away. Why?*

"You remember Cousin Arabella." There was no question in her mother's whispery voice, just one of her countless charms. "You were always her favorite. And how convenient that she should invite you at this time. The Columbia Territory—"

The pale-blue stationery fluttered from Mother's slender, ringed fingers—coming to rest in a pool of soft lamplight that formed a halo on the deep pile of the carpet. The stationery was familiar. Cousin Arabella always used blue paper in her seldom letters. And the message this time was the reason for Mother's summons.

"She is in need of a companion," Ana Glamora said without meeting her daughter's eyes. "It seems—well, that the experience will be good now that you're out of school..."

The whispery voice trailed off a little uncertainly, then resumed again. Mother was uncomfortable with silence. "Of course, you will not feel lonely—her being a distant relative—"

Distant? Yes. Cousin Arabella, whom Courtney had not seen since her father's funeral, she hardly remembered. That was eight years ago, when she was only eight. She did recall mention of the relative who lived "Out West," but that could mean anywhere. Anyway, that kind of distance had nothing to do with Mrs. Glamora's meaning. *Distant* had to do with bloodline. The family stopped counting beyond third cousins those who married "beneath the fine Virginia stock," which, supposedly, dated back to royalty.

Coming slowly back into the universe, Courtney was aware of the ghostly tap-tap-tap of an ice-tipped shrub against the stained-glass panel of the parlor window. It was still winter here. But she recalled Cousin Arabella's describing her home in that strange place to which she referred to as "the land of eternal spring." This meant that trains, stagecoaches, or whatever transportation her mother had in mind would be running, Courtney supposed.

But why was she being bundled away so hurriedly? Not because of Lance Sterling, surely! Why, the two of them had known each other since birth. Maybe someday...someday a long, long time away. . . but even if romance bloomed between them, they would have their families' blessings. All were "aristocrats."

"Why, Mother?" Courtney's voice was as ghostly as the icy fingers of the tapping shrub.

"Why, uh, Courtney—" Ana Glamora hesitated. Was she so preoccupied as to forget her daughter's name? "I expected you to view this as a great adventure—the way Vanessa looked upon the London Theatre of Arts—and Efraim, his admittance to Harvard. Please don't choose to be difficult."

Mother always thought her difficult, Courtney realized sadly as she concentrated on the pattern of the Persian rug. Efraim, eldest of the three Glamora children (named for his maternal grandfather and Courtney's idol) went obediently to the university, but not before telling her secretly that he had little interest in perpetuating the English culture and that he (with his characteristic lopsided grin) personally would swap books for buckskins when he graduated. Wide-eyed, she listened as he promised that the two of them would escape this pretentious life and hide away in the Portland wilderness. That meant Maine to Courtney. . . only Cousin Arabella mentioned Portland as if it were Out West. It was all very confusing.

"Vanessa needs me for one thing—and—"

Now fully aware that her mother was holding something back, Courtney waited and thought about her older sister, who was Mother's favorite. Small wonder, when she was so beautiful and so talented. She was an exact replica of their mother, while the dark-eyed Courtney was a throwback to what Mother referred to (with some disdain) as the "other side."

Slowly, Courtney raised tragic eyes, much too large for the oval face, to study the row of English ancestors that lined the walls of the great room. "Bluebloods" every one of them, Mother said—all from *her* side of the family. Looking away from their disapproving stares, her gaze caught her own eyes in the corridor mirror. Smooth, dark hair—parted demurely in the middle and hanging loosely far below her shoulders . . . wearing a plain dress of dark blue with white collar and cuffs, she was plain . . . plain . . . *plain*! Not only was she unlovely, but she lacked the brilliance of Efraim and the artistic aptitudes of Vanessa. A finishing school was appropriate for her youngest, Mother had said, and promptly sent her away "to where you can be with girls your own age."

Forcing her eyes past the ancestors, Courtney looked at her mother—or was it Vanessa? "The beautiful Mrs. Glamora," people said of her golden-goddess face. And, invariably, the comment was followed by, "And her daughter is just as lovely—her older daughter, that is."

Efraim looked somewhat like their mother too, in a masculine sort of way. His blond good looks would win him any case if he changed his mind about the buckskins. But there the resemblance ended. His personality was that of their father—a man remembered for his towering goodness. Unconsciously, Courtney sighed. It was she who inherited Father's quiet humility and his dark coloring—maybe also a bit of his "dark side" (the phrase Ana Glamora used to describe her husband's moods).

And truly there were times when Gabriel ("Big Gabe") Glamora sat reading his Bible, meditating with his eyes closed; and then, when he opened them, he was lost in thought—maybe even despondency, Courtney realized now—until he looked at his gold-of-hair, perfect-of-complexion wife. "Lady Ana," he called her (pronouncing her name Ah-na). Remembering Father made Courtney wish she were a little girl again—curled up in his lap, safe, listening to his Bible stories in which the saints addressed one another as "Mate" or "Love." He would never have sent her away. How different her life would have been! But there had been a deadly cave-in at the coal mine, coming at a time when, as owner, he was in the bowels of darkness inspecting for the safety of his workers. Courtney remembered shutting herself in a dark closet, pretending it was the mine, and wishing with all her heart the walls would cave in on her too. Through the closed door she heard words—words that had no meaning. *Yes, Mrs. Glamora, you are protected. Yes, the entire fortune is yours—except for...* Mr. Levitt, the attorney, lowered his voice confidentially. Hours later, it seemed, the man went away, leaving Courtney to grieve—and Mother an heiress.

"So it is settled," Mother said now, as she had said then. Only this time she was sending Courtney away. Into the unknown...

CHAPTER 2
Strange Departure

There was a small flurry of excitement, Courtney admitted to herself, in preparing for this journey that all other goings-away had lacked. The land into which she was going was as mysterious as the why of the long trek, whereas the other trips were closer and in "civilized country." But, as Maj, the tight-lipped maid who claimed to speak little English but was all ears when others spoke, helped her pack, Courtney found the situation more and more puzzling. That her mother, who perpetuated the English way of life, should send her into the Columbia Country filled with "uncivilized ruffians and red-skinned barbarians" simply made no sense.

"Why, Maj?" Courtney asked as she had asked Mother.

The maid fingered an English tweed suit she was laying out for traveling. " 'Cause she—beg pardon, Miss—her *Ladyship* be plannin'—" Maj, caught off guard, began. Then, her strong features coloring, she stopped as if using a forbidden tongue.

Perhaps it was the reassuring pat that Courtney gave the girl's arm that prompted her to bring Efraim's dog-eared books and some roughly sketched maps of the indescribably beautiful chain of mountains known as the Cascades in the Oregon Territory and the Sierra Nevada in California. Beautiful. But, she shivered, dangerous. Threatening. How on earth could one cross them? And once inside their lock, how would one escape? Courtney looked at the maps again. The mountains, like her trip, seemed to hold some secret. Maybe someday she would be able to unlock both.

Mother stayed out of sight as the preparations were made and the day of departure drew frighteningly near. But Lance came.

Dear, dear Lance. He was genuinely shocked by her news. "You mean your mother is actually sending you away—so far? That it's all settled?"

The boy's luminous eyes no longer teased. They were pools of thought, and for a moment Courtney thought his tapered, patrician hands were going to touch her. That would be nice—nice to have *somebody* care. But the moment was lost when his hands fell awkwardly to his sides. A hated black curl fell over his high forehead, and his eyes resumed their look of recklessness.

"I will come to visit you!" Lance promised rashly.

That was the first Courtney had given thought to the length of her stay in the faraway land. It was the first time, too, that she had thought of Lance as anything more than a childhood playmate. But now, with his eyes burning into hers, she no longer saw him as only a year older than herself. He was all grown up, had finished his studies in English literature, and had become the artist he always dreamed of being. What was more, Courtney felt herself fleshing to young maidenhood. And, in her new image, she watched the gangling youth of their yesterdays mature. For one magical moment she endowed him with noble qualities. Napoleon, the Conquerer . . . Rembrandt, the Painter . . . and Lance —*of course*, Sir Lancelot, the Lover!

Lance may have shared her feelings. Or perhaps he muscled into the hero he saw in her eyes. Whatever the motivation, he gallantly reached for her small hand and held it to his lips briefly in a first caress. Then, red-faced, he raced away—stumbling over the hedge he intended to leap.

The nostalgic moment helped Courtney through the impersonal goodbye of her mother and the wave of premature homesickness that engulfed her as she and Mrs. Thorpe boarded the family coach, bound for the train station. Mrs. Thorpe ("Nanny" to the Glamora children whom she had served as governess and surrogate mother since their birth) would accompany her to the Continental Divide, by prearrangement. There Courtney was to meet Cousin Arabella's housekeeper, Mrs. Rueben, who would "properly chaperone" her. It was lucky the woman was visiting her children in Colorado, Mrs. Thorpe said, but unlucky that the woman spoke no English.

Courtney found neither good fortune nor bad in either case. She was too crushed over her most recent exile.

Mrs. Thorpe seemed to understand. Ordinarily she was undemonstrative, but as the carriage rolled away and Courtney strained her neck hoping for a glimpse of her mother waving a farewell, the large, capable woman reached her hand from beneath her black cape and touched Courtney's.

"Don't look back, my child—don't ever look back—just look ahead to the adventure of it all. In a way," she said with a hint of sadness in her usually strict voice, "I wish I were going all the way."

"When will I meet Cousin Arabella—and where?" Courtney's voice quavered. She knew so little about the trip.

"In Portland. At least, that is the arrangement."

The train heaved mightily, hissed, and moved backward, then forward, as if trying to decide the proper direction. Then, slowly, there was the grind of steel against steel as the wheels turned over and over. In their slow-forward rhythm there was a mocking singsong, *Unwanted. . . unwanted. . . unfit*!

Unaware that others had turned to glimpse the slight young thing so resembling a Renaissance Madonna, Courtney turned toward the window to hide her tears. She watched the receding landscape of home grow smaller and then disappear. Somehow she knew that she would never see Waverly Manor again. What about Mother, Efraim, Vanessa—and Lance? The lump in her throat enlarged. *Never* was such a dreadful word. . .

CHAPTER 3
The Truth—In Part

Courtney moved restlessly on the scratchy upholstery of the train seat. She had never enjoyed traveling, and this trip was taking forever. How long had they been en route, anyway? She had lost count. She tried to concentrate on the slow-moving scenery through the coal-blackened window but found little of interest. She was stiff, sore, and so filled with homesickness that she wondered if the disease was fatal.

All too soon the railway led her and Mrs. Thorpe away from the smoky hills and misty valleys, through the last of the verdant forests, and into wastelands. There were only a few houses, which looked more like caves, on the vast prairie—some wheat, she supposed it was, but it was trampled down by the frequent herds of buffalo that stampeded away from the huffing and heaving of the train. They changed trains several times, with an occasional layover, but Mrs. Thorpe all but covered Courtney's eyes with her cape, so afraid was she that her precious charge would see or be seen. One never knew about strange men, she cautioned over and over.

Nanny meant well. Courtney shuddered at the thought of saying goodbye to her. Nanny was the only security she had known since her father's death. To keep from dwelling on the parting, Courtney reflected on her background—what she knew . . . and what she did not. Quite possibly this would be a good time to question Nanny—maybe the last opportunity.

She was aware of constant conflict which had gone on between the Glamoras and the Bellevues for generations. Money versus title—and, in the case of Courtney's parents, Glamora wealth versus Bellevue beauty. Her great-grandfathers had been business associates in Europe—if one could call it that. Grandsire Bellevue was the major stockholder in some kind of import-export business while Grandfather Glamora was a mere shopkeeper (looked down upon by the upper class—second only to the peasantry). With the Bellevues holding the advantage of both wealth and title, they shunned the Glamoras. When the business failed, the stockholders decided that it was nobler to be among the "genteel poor" than resort to labor. With chins held high, somehow they were unaware that the shops thrived by other means and that the Glamoras came into "money without power." A total outrage! On that the great-grandfathers agreed.

Then something awful happened—something *terribly* awful, Nanny told Courtney once in a weak moment. Nobody knew the details of the dispute, just that it resulted in a sunrise duel. While neither of the ancestors was killed, both were badly injured.

One of them (Courtney could never remember which) lost a limb and hobbled on a pegleg whittled by a cobbler. The other was bedridden with paralysis from a bullet lodged in his spine.

After that, disdain turned to hatred. The Bellevues could never forgive a Commoners's having prospered while they, direct descendants of the Queen of England, failed. They clung to their titles as a drowning man of the sea clutches at a splinter from a sinking ship. And, when at length both families migrated to America, they brought along their grudges. Even as the hostile clans went their separate ways, marrying out of the Glamoras and the Bellevues until there was no "pure strain" remaining, the hatred lingered. At the very mention of each other's name, both sides bristled.

Until Father and Mother—

"How did my parents come to marry?" Courtney's question, born of her thinking, surprised her as much as Nanny.

Mrs. Thorpe, who had just returned from an attempted walk down the narrow aisle of the coach, sat down heavily. "Conductor ordered me to my chair," she said. "Guess he's right. Knotted muscles are to be preferred over a broken hip. Seems we're getting into some mountains."

Sure enough, the train was creaking as if with rheumatism as it snaked up the foothills toward a series of snowcapped peaks. Courtney turned her eyes from the scene, lovely as it was, to meet those of Mrs. Thorpe. They were red-rimmed. The pass ahead looked frightening, but Nanny would never cry over possible danger. More likely, as the train seemed to have turned northward, she realized that the journey would be ending soon and she would lose her "baby."

And so it was that she gave Courtney her first straight answer concerning her parents' union.

"Your grandfather Glamora was an enterprising man. Put down like that by his betters was the motivation he needed, I guess. Some men are like that, you know—"

No, she didn't know. There was very little Courtney did know about men, leading a sheltered life of near-imprisonment. But she waited wordlessly lest the spell be broken and she never learn the secrets of her past.

Mrs. Thorpe wiped her eyes, handed Courtney an apple from her paisley bag, and continued: "As I heard it, the man went into coal mining—divided his time between saving enough money to bring him to America and teaching his children to choose their mates with care. His dying wish was for descendants who could put the likes of the Bellevues to shame!"

Courtney listened, wide-eyed with fascination. "And my father?" She whispered when Mrs. Thorpe paused to bite into her own apple. Courtney's lay in her lap untouched.

"Eat your fruit!" Mrs. Thorpe demanded, and waited until Courtney bit into the apple.

"Well, some said your grandfather denied his children everything but their daily bread and books—fitting them to be on the intellectual level of the upper class and demanding that every friend of either gender be screened by him personally."

"He sounds cruel," Courtney said, more to herself than her companion.

Mrs. Thorpe swallowed the last of her apple, held

the core up gingerly, then tossed it into the nearest spittoon. "Not cruel—more like ambitious. Smart, too, to realize that money alone's not enough. One needed a cultured mind to attract the well-bred, court and wed them, then create *family*—meaning if not nobility in family, at least not peasantry!"

Courtney let her unfinished apple fall into the folds of her long tweed skirt. "But why did Grandfather Glamora find quarrel with labor as the Bellevues? Father said work was noble."

Mrs. Thorpe pressed the cushion-tips of her large fingers together and pointed her hands upward as if in search of divine guidance. At length she sighed. "So it is, according to your father's philosophy. But we are speaking of *nobility*—something he lacked. But he was a fine gentleman!" She said loyally.

"But my parents?" Courtney said, bringing the subject back to her original question.

The train coughed out a wheezy warning as it labored around a hairpin curve and Nanny's possible answer was lost. Courtney's mind was busy with the strange turn of events. While the Glamoras with their "new money" prepared the offspring to seek gentry, the Bellevues—new penniless—instructed their own in the art of attracting wealthy mates.

"Well-prepared," Nanny had said. Yes, Mother was well-prepared. Her breeding and bloodline placed her at the top of the list of eligible mates—if one must be so cold-blooded. Courtney shuddered as the ugly phrase of "fortune hunter" came unbidden.

"How did Father make his money?" she asked in a small voice as the train strained to a near-halt.

"He knew coal. Every man has his Achilles' heel. Work was your father's. It was almost as if he knew someone as beautiful would come his way—although—"

Mrs. Thorpe halted her sentence as if to check the time on the enameled watch pinned to her shirt-waist blouse...an excuse for not completing the sentence. Everyone knew trains followed no schedule.

"Although what, Nanny? The marriage had to be approved by both families—was it *arranged*?" The last word died in Courtney's throat. Something else in her was dying too.

"Well, yes—but your father adored your beautiful mother, just as he adored *you*. Now put the matter to rest, my child—"

Courtney hardly heard. "How did they ever get together, the two families—hating one another as they did?"

Mrs. Thorpe was picking up her bag. "There was a terrible scene—rivaling that of their fathers before them...and, sad to say, no reconciliation afterward, no *Romeo and Juliet* ending. The hatred continues to this day, a burning that neither fire nor water can quench. Best be locating your things, Courtney. We must be almost there."

Courtney nodded obediently, her mind on the past. It was easy to imagine the exchange between her grandfathers. The injured pride. The gloating mingled with unyielding inferiority. The guilt. And the hate—the awful hate that neither war nor love could end. One look at the ancestral lineup of ancient photographs gave Courtney an insight on their personalities. Grandfather Glamora (pushed insignificantly into a corner as if he did not belong in his son's house) still managed to dominate the scene. His dark eyes studied the deep mahogany of the furniture with a look of pride, giving him a sense of belonging that life had failed to give him. And Grandfather Bellevue, his delicate coloring so light that it seemed to fade into the wallpaper, looking as if poised for flight when the conversation at hand was closed. The *arrangement*? But what had any of this to do with Courtney's being sent away now?

"Nanny, *please*—" she began. But the train had stopped. And, even before the passengers rose from their seats, Mrs. Thorpe's eyes were searching for Courtney's chaperone.

CHAPTER 4

Unsuitable Chaperone

Courtney pulled her heavy shawl snugly around her thin shoulders. The mountain air was stimulating but brisk. Cinder-studded smoke still puffed from the stack of the tired engine, sweeping upward then earthward to engulf the exhausted travelers. Courtney wiped at a cinder in her eye, then swept a gloved hand over her stinging face. Unaware that her entire face was streaked with soot, she looked in awe at the scenery around them while Mrs. Thorpe searched for someone resembling a proper chaperone.

Evergreens, singly and in groves, surrounded the area. And between them stood clusters of aspen, still pure and white in late-spring nudity. Snow had melted on the level ground, giving way to a carpet of wildflowers. But beyond, the snow-bonneted mountains touched the sky. Lance would love painting here. Oh, there was so much to tell him! And Efraim—yes, Efraim would love the untamed land. Courtney hoped the Lord had created the Columbia

Country as beautifully . . . that it was like the Garden her father told her about . . . and the Serpent had not found it . . .

Buried so deep in her thinking, Courtney failed to notice the touch of a hand on her arm until the fingers tightened slightly and a rich male voice said pleasantly, "Miss Glamora?"

Courtney's heart jumped into her throat. This man was a stranger. Young ladies did not speak to strangers, Nanny said . . . and where in the world *was* Nanny?

Frantic, her eyes turned toward the small, weathered train depot she had glimpsed only slightly as Nanny searched for their baggage. And the buildings—were they there before? They appeared to be only storefronts, hastily erected or hastily abandoned. Well-protected in the rear by the mountain chain and fenced in by forests were the beginnings or the endings of a town. Neatly designed foundations of native rock formed a rectangle in the center, and around it was a great circle of weathered-log squares, intended perhaps for homes. Then the buildings blurred and Courtney's head spun like a carousel . . . whirling at impossible speed . . . tilting her forward toward the horrible scene her eyes had missed before. The charred remains of a wagon train! So it was true—there *were* hostile Indians . . .

Her heart was pounding unmercifully when she turned full-face to the man who continued to hold her arm. Her vision had not cleared and her mouth felt stuffed with down.

"Who—who are you?" Courtney's tongue was thick, but she pulled herself full-height in an effort to regain her composure.

Even so, the top of her head reached only to his wide, plaid shoulders. When she tilted her face upward, Courtney met a pair of the bluest eyes she had ever seen—lakes, they were, lakes in which one could drown, as she was doing now. Tall . . . lean . . . lithe . . . without an ounce of superfluous flesh . . . skin made copper by sun and wind. The horror of the charred scene and her fear of the stranger faded as Courtney's eyes traveled over the face above her. The sun-bronzed hair beneath the wide brim of his felt hat had a rebellious kink. His nose was clean-cut. Fascinated by the jawline, Courtney allowed her eyes to linger on the formidable strength of purpose she read there.

"Do I pass inspection?" There was amusement in the deep voice.

Courtney felt hot color stain her cheeks. "I don't know what you mean, I'm sure."

And then the incredible happened. The stranger burst into laughter. "I beg your pardon, Miss Glamora—because surely that's who you are—but you should see your face. Here, let me fix it for you."

And before Courtney could object, he had drawn an enormous bandanna from his pocket and was wiping away the mess the cinders had made. And, suddenly, looking up into those blue, blue lakes lighted with ripples of amusement, Courtney found herself laughing too.

It was thus that Mrs. Thorpe found them. And for a moment the woman was speechless. Courtney, her sad-faced little Courtney, was laughing? Why, it was all she herself could do to coax a smile into those pensive eyes. And laughing with a stranger! But she knew her duty. This had to stop *now*. How dare this forward young man!

Raising her parasol as if to strike him, Mrs. Thorpe marched to stand beside him. "Take your hands off this young lady who is in my charge before I call the conductor! Who *are* you and where are your manners?"

Still smiling, the handsome stranger wiped a last cinder from Courtney's forehead before answering. Then, bowing slightly, he said, "My name is Clinton Desmond—a cousin, in a sense, of Miss Courtney Glamora."

"Don't be impertinent, young man!" Mrs. Thorpe sniffed. "In a sense, indeed! Either you are a cousin or you aren't."

"Well, you see, Mrs. Thorpe—you are Mrs. Thorpe, aren't you?—I am Aunt Arabella's half-sister's son by her third husband. You must admit it is somewhat complicated."

Courtney found it difficult to keep a straight face. Just who the charming stranger was or why he was here made little difference. She had never met anyone she enjoyed more.

"That tells me nothing. I shall need to find Mrs. Rueben to accompany Miss Glamora and explain matters—"

"Mrs. Rueben will be along shortly. But as to explaining—perhaps you were unaware she speaks only German—"

Mrs. Thorpe snorted. "Then state your business!"

Clinton Desmond was all business now. Pulling himself to an even greater height, he said politely, "I can understand your concern, Mrs. Thorpe. Aunt Arabella—Miss Kennedy—would share it. Meeting this young lady was one of her reasons for timing the shipment as she did. You see, there have been several attempted holdups, and she wanted me along to protect the silver—and Miss Glamora in case—"

"I find you a totally unsuitable chaperone!" Mrs. Thorpe said stiffly.

Clinton Desmond's eyes met Courtney's over the determined woman's head. In those blue, blue lakes Courtney saw the twinkle return, and she responded by biting her lower lip to suppress a smile. *He knows,* Courtney thought, *just as I know that Nanny's bark is worse than her bite!*

Mrs. Rueben, a little wrenlike woman, made her appearance, and acknowledged Clinton Desmond's introductions (from behind heaps of bundles done up in squares of burlap) with something akin to "*Ach!*" Mrs. Thorpe eyed her suspiciously, but there was a warning whistle of the Northern Pacific, which had brought her and Courtney on the last lap. Now it was time to part. Everyone was talking at once. Villard's Special to Portland was waiting too. Passengers bound both east and west were gathering belongings, bidding farewell to travelers met on the way, and scurrying their opposite directions. Courtney welcomed the confusion. It saved her from the sentimental goodbye she had dreaded. "Oh, Nanny, I love you, I love you!" she longed to cry out. But that would only prolong the agony of parting. Mrs. Thorpe's embrace, too, was restrained. Tears were for later.

"Don't look back," Nanny had said, so Courtney looked straight ahead as Clint Desmond, his arms piled high with the housekeeper's bundles, led the way to the spur where their train waited. Thank goodness, Courtney thought, her own trunks would be taken care of by the crew.

The two engineers, their faces black with cinders —having caught up on the "back home" news from each other—signaled to the conductors. And Courtney found herself being helped aboard the train which would take her to the strange new world. She felt a mixture of excitement and dread. After all, what did she know of Cousin Arabella? She found an unexplainable security in knowing that Clinton Desmond would present her. In fact, she was glad he was going to be with her all the way. Nanny was entitled to her opinion, but, secretly, Courtney found him a suitable chaperone indeed!

Courtney blushed a little self-consciously—hoping her new acquaintance was unable to read her thoughts—as he seated her near the window. Using the soot-darkened reflection as a mirror, she adjusted her blue velvet bonnet. Mrs. Rueben plopped herself between them. And again the smile of understanding between Courtney and her new "chaperone."

CHAPTER 5
Dream Country

Crossing the prairies with their vast lands of nothingness and laboring up the Rocky Mountains had brought a myriad of discomfort, boredom, and sadness. Nanny had complained constantly about the lack of air, boxed in as they were with only dust, soot, and stale smoke that managed to make its way from the men's smoker. When she was not complaining, she was fussing over Courtney. Her suit was wrinkled. She looked as pale as a sheet. Was she feeling poorly?

"I'm fine, just fine," Courtney had assured Mrs. Thorpe so many times that she felt like a parrot.

Courtney was no whiner. Wealth had made no dent in her personality. Neither had social position. The only dent sprang from the need of love and approval that her mother withheld. But she had grown to accept it as a part of her life, unaware that it lent to her face the sad-sweet Madonna look that others found so appealing. But when she smiled, it was as if the sunshine broke through the clouds for a brief moment. And when she laughed, which was seldom, there was the chime of Christmas bells—rare because of its infrequency and beautiful because of the silvery notes that so few people heard. Clinton Desmond was among them when he wiped her sooty face.

Remembering made Courtney smile again as the train creaked and moaned and then lurched forward. The trip from here on would be different. They would be descending—far safer, she thought in her inexperience—and she would have an interesting companion. And the landscape would be *beautiful*—if Efraim's books had it right.

Her mind began to cloud with fanciful dreams. She found herself wondering if she had brought along suitable clothes . . . an assortment of feathered and veiled millinery . . . velvet cloak . . . dove-gray doeskin gloves that Vanessa had sent from London for her birthday . . . and the French lace mitts that Efraim had ordered from Paris. She had an assortment of lovely gowns in case Cousin Arabella had a ball in her honor . . .

Clinton Desmond interrupted her thinking. "You will find us very informal here on the frontier—so may I call you Courtney? And you, in turn, must call me Clint."

"Yes, Clint," she said obediently, little realizing how demure she sounded. Feeling shy, she busied herself removing the button-down blue gloves that Nanny had deemed proper.

Clint watched. "You have lovely hands," he said quietly.

Courtney examined her tapering, white fingers as if seeing them for the first time. "These I inherited from Mother," she said as if making a discovery.

"The rest of me is pure Glamora. I—"

She paused. What must he think of her? Going on like this with a man she had just met? And what about Mrs. Rueben? But Mrs. Rueben heard nothing, saw nothing, and spoke nothing. Her whole attention was on the enormous shawl she was knitting, her thin lips keeping time with the clicking of the flying needles, obviously trying to complete as many stitches as possible before daylight faded. Already the sun was setting in a blaze of crimson glory and a few belated birds winged swiftly against the Western sky. To her right, the forest shadows lengthened, then merged into a single pattern. Above them the stars came out one by one, flickered uncertainly, then shone with steady brilliancy. The train jerked, hissed warningly, and shuddered as if in pain, breaking the spell. Then, as if pleased with itself, it picked up speed—only to grind to a halt that all but sent the conductor standing on his head.

Clint reached across Mrs. Rueben and touched Courtney's hand. "Are you all right? It will be like this all the way down, I'm afraid—but, oh, the beauty! I will show as much as possible to you tomorrow and fill you in on the history of what I privately term Dream Country!"

Courtney smiled with pleasure. *Tomorrow... tomorrow...* her eyes grew heavy and her head drooped. Did she only imagine Clint's removing her bonnet and smoothing her hair? Anything could happen in Dream Country...

CHAPTER 6
Providence of God

Night yielded to morning. The rosy fingers of dawn poked through the tall trees. Mrs. Rueben was dozing, still gripping her knitting needles. But the seat beside her was empty. Courtney, aware of a gnawing in her stomach, examined her reflection in the smoke-streaked window. She looked exhausted. Small wonder after the endless days and nights of traveling! Her backbone was rubbed raw from slumping against the hard seats and her insides were rebelling at the diet of stale muffins and shriveled fruit—not to mention the constant jerking and jolting of this westbound train as the engineer strained with all his might to prevent a runaway. Oh, for a warm bath, a change of clothes, a place to brush her teeth! And, oh, for a slice of warm toast . . . a coddled egg . . .

For a fleeting moment Courtney wondered if her mother had any idea how different this kind of travel was from the Eastern railroads. Trains there had powder rooms, diners . . .

"At your service, Miss!" Clint stood beside her. "I bribed the engineer. If you can manage to slip past our sleeping chaperone, we will share this feast. On this side we will have a view—"

Stifling a giggle, Courtney—with the help of Clint's hand—was already scuttling sideways over the sleeping woman's sensible, high-topped, lace-up shoes. Clint helped her across the aisle as the train hissed and came to a near-stop. She all but lost her footing, then tumbled into the seat beside the window. Clint nearly fell on top of her, but neither noticed.

"Oh—oh, *Clint*!" Courtney gasped when she looked below. "That has to be the most *beautiful* river in North America!"

"Yes, I think the most beautiful," Clint said, easing his great frame into the seat beside her. It's fed by the melting glaciers and leads to the Pacific Ocean. But, here, eat your breakfast before it's cold."

Courtney turned reluctantly from the churning waters. Coffee, *hot* coffee—and an egg . . . and something resembling a biscuit spread with marmalade . . .

"Where—how?" Already she was stuffing her mouth with food, which might have been somewhat flat but to her was a feast. Courtney attacked the egg, unaware of Clint's grin of amusement. There was marmalade on her small nose, and now, in her haste for a hot drink, she had sloshed coffee down the front of her once-white but now-soiled blouse.

"I know the right people," Clint said, trying to wipe away the grin. "I make this trip often—silver for Aunt Arabella's mines. The men bring some grub and grab other at watering tanks if there's a place. They heat it on—"

But Courtney failed to hear the rest of his sentence. She had seen his look of amusement and felt hot color stain her cheeks. What in the world must he think of her? And where were her boarding school manners? Why, young ladies *never* appeared hungry! It was vulgar, crude, and totally unacceptable in polite society. Miss Adelaide had compelled the girls to eat a small snack before attending any function where there would be food—to stave off any appearance of hunger. And here she had eaten like a glutton! What was more, she had given no thought whatever to Clinton Desmond. And they were supposed to *share.*

But Clinton Desmond did not mind in the slightest. Gently he wiped away the remnants of food from her face and apologized for the lack of napkins. What a gentleman!

And suddenly they were again sharing a laugh. Then Clint was pointing below at the river, explaining its power and how it supplied almost all the people in the Columbia Territory. Once the river was called the Oregon—

Why the change? she wondered, draining the tin cup.

When the states divided, it seemed inappropriate. As a matter of fact, for some reason the legislature decided to change the more poetic name of Columbia to Washington in honor of the first President. But most of the settlers clung to the name—and to Clint, it was Dream Country.

"How did anyone find such country?" Courtney was turning her head to look at the vine-entwined evergreens which formed a steep cliff to their right, then back to the sheer drop below where the beautiful river formed swirling rapids. "How did Cousin

Arabella come to be here?"

Would he think her questions foolish? Courtney was unaccustomed to anybody giving her an audience. But this man was as different as the land around them. She had a feeling he would answer if she asked the question as to why he was not frightened in spite of their dangerous downhill stop-and-go speed—and the even more dangerous possibilities that lay ahead. But Clint was answering as if her questions were downright brilliant, something which set her heart to racing and changed her grave face to a starry-eyed beauty.

"As to our relative, Courtney," he smiled, "—she prefers 'Bella,' by the way—well, her ancestors came with some of the first wagon trains—over this very route, incidentally. Oh, no railroads," Clint explained, reading the question in her eyes, "but over the Applegate Trail. The railroad follows it as close as was practical . . . and someday, not in our time perhaps, but sometime there will undoubtedly be a scenic highway through here—"

Fascinated, Courtney listened as he told of their common ancestors and explained their hardships and their ultimate triumphs in hacking their way through a wilderness and taming it.

"Of course, it was the mining business that made the Kennedys wealthy—namely, Aunt Bella's father. There were ore, coal, copper, and silver. The silver was most valuable, but then, I am sure you knew this?"

Clint's statement was a question, so Courtney shook her head. There was really so little she did know. And she was relieved when he went back to her original question concerning the first explorers.

"As to how the land came to be discovered, there are theories and there are fragments of truth. I personally have a strong conviction in the providence of God. You see, for two centuries ships had been searching for the Great River of the West, a passageway to the Atlantic—those who had sailed our shores. Everybody looked. But nobody saw! Fogs hid the mighty Columbia . . . sickness struck down the crews . . . or storms drove them aside. God Himself had withheld the prize of the Columbia River Valley—until the time was right—"

"God, Clint?"

"Yes, God, Courtney."

Clint had the good sense to let her consider the God she had not heard mentioned since the death of Father. And then not in these terms. She bit her lip and said slowly, "Do you think this is the way He works?"

Clint touched Courtney's hand and his blue eyes had become more blue in their intensity. "I am convinced of it deep in my heart. God has a hand in everything—everything that is *good* and for His purpose." He inhaled deeply. "I pray that you will come to understand this . . . for it was He who brought you here."

CHAPTER 7
Innisfree

The train lurched forward, then slowed sickeningly like a wheel at the top of its climb that was suddenly dropping downward. Instinctively, Courtney reached and found Clint's protective hands. Maybe they were going to derail and drown in the river below. She sought Clint's eyes for reassurance. But they were fastened on the scene below, and there was a look of near-reverence on his countenance—profound respect mingled with love and awe.

"Look, my darling," he whispered, and Courtney knew that in the otherworldliness of his mind the words had slipped out unconsciously. And suddenly she was there with him.

They were two people alone in a crowd. Only the two of them saw the miracle of the broad plateau below—the giant mass of snowclad peaks surrounded by dense virgin evergreens, some of them entwined with vines so tightly woven that no sun could penetrate the darkness of the rain forest. . . some almost inaccessible, all irregular. It was an artist's paradise, a patchwork of deep, mysterious valleys bulwarked with high ridges and glacier-carrying peaks. . . snowfields. . . alpine meadows splashed with the pastels of wildflowers . . . clear lakes, like Clint's eyes, winking in unexpected places. . . cascades of sparkling water falling from great heights to join the brimming river. *Dream Country indeed.*

Courtney broke the silence at last. "Oh, Clint, it's beautiful. You are right—Washington seems the wrong name for it."

Clint squeezed her hand in appreciation. "But we all have our private places in the heart, places where we store our sacred thoughts. I was thinking of the lovely name 'Innisfree.' That's Donolar's name for it—from his private world—"

" 'Innisfree'—I love Yeats' poem—but Donolar?"

"You haven't heard about him yet? I thought Aunt Bella would have told you." Clint met her eyes, and there she saw something unreadable, but she did not question. Cousin Bella would tell her all she needed to know. Instead, she said:

> "I will arise and go now, and go to
> Innisfree. . ."

Clint picked up the next line with her, and together they continued the poem:

> And a small cabin build there, of clay and
> wattles made:
> Nine bean rows will I have there, a hive
> for the honey bee,
> And live alone in the bee-loud glade.

And I shall have some peace there, for
  peace comes dropping slow
Dropping from the veils of the morning to
  where the cricket sings:
There midnight's all a glimmer, and moon
  a purple glow,
And evening full of the linnets' wings. . .

Clint suddenly stopped, dropped Courtney's hand, and put a silencing finger to his lips. The train had come to a screeching halt. And outside there was a volley of shots. . .

CHAPTER 8
Holdup!

Mrs. Rueben was the first of the passengers to let out an alarm. Although it was in German, her tone alerted the others to impending danger.

"Holdup!" men, women, and children chorused as they bolted from their seats and trampled one another in search of some means of escape. There was none.

It was Clint who brought a semblance of order. "Sit down, everyone," he said quietly but with a command in his voice. "Obviously, the men are bandits," he went on, tilting his head toward the windows on the east, "but remember that none of your possessions are worth your life!"

Obediently the passengers returned to their seats, scrambling over one another, and pointing wildly to where a crowd of men on horseback sat, their faces obscured with bandannas and their guns pointed directly at the stalled train.

"Stay as calm as you can, Courtney. You will be needed. It's the payroll they're after—and thank

God, I don't have it!" Clint whispered just as the bandits entered the coach.

The masked men waved guns and shouted orders. Even through the heavy bandannas that fluttered in and out with their breathing, Courtney could smell the scent of stale smoke and alcohol. There was little telling what they would do if they were sober. Drunk, they were less than animals.

"Okay, folks, she's a stickup. Ante up 'n ye mightn't git hurt. Otherwise, it'll be my pleasure—"

The speaker was brandishing his gun in the face of an old, old man whose face was florid with anger. "Th' Almighty'll git ye, He will, iffen ye take me Bible—"

"We dun want no Good Book, ole man—be emptyin' them pockets. That's it—dump 'er right here in th' hat—"

For a moment Courtney watched in horrible fascination. Then she turned to check on Mrs. Rueben, whose protests rose shrilly above the enraged bandit who was trying to jerk a gold chain, from which dangled a cross, from her neck. Without thinking, Courtney slipped from her seat and crawled across the aisle to the woman's rescue. To her horror, she saw that Mrs. Rueben's face had turned blue and blood was oozing from where the chain had cut into her neck.

"Stop it, you brute! Can't you see you're killing her?" Then, remembering Clint's warning, she quickly unclasped the chain and dropped the treasured cross into the hat—her heart filled with remorse and, for the first time in her life, something akin to hatred.

"Thank ye, sweet face! And now it's yore turn—"

"I have nothing of value," Courtney said, trying

to keep her voice steady. What she said was true. Mother loved jewelry, but it was always for herself. Later, for Vanessa and Courtney, she promised, a promise that meant little to Courtney.

"Be gittin' that chain off'n that purty neck, less'n ye want a bullet through it."

The locket he meant! She had forgotten about the one piece of jewelry she owned, a locket with a picture of her father—his last gift to her. No, no. . .but Clint had said. . .

"Forgive me, Father," she whispered—wondering if she was addressing her earthly father or the heavenly One that Clint seemed to know so much about. Holding back the tears, she dropped the precious locket into the hat and turned her attention to Mrs. Rueben—patting her wrists and fanning her with her handkerchief. She was so white. Could she be dead?

Courtney felt for a pulse, but her own fingers were shaking so badly that she was unable to tell if there was movement. Frantic, she raised her eyes in search of Clint. He was standing statue-still at the front end of the coach which led to the baggage room, and there was cold fury written on his face. Oh, surely he would do nothing foolish. . .try and stop the robbers. . .

She heard his voice, low and powerful. "Only a coward would use a gun on unarmed people." His bravery frightened Courtney.

And with good reason! The man pushed the muzzle of the gun to Clint's temple. "Remember, you asked for it, Desmond!"

"Stop! Don't you dare hurt him!"

The scream was out before Courtney knew it was coming. And somebody must have put wings on her heels, for she was between Clint and the would-be murderer, her tiny body like a straw attempting to protect a fortress.

She heard Clint's gasp of horror. And then there was bedlam. Never would she remember. Passengers leaped from their seats and, almost as if by plan, divided into groups to attack the bandits. Taken by surprise, the two who stood guard at the back of the coach were at a disadvantage. They hesitated one moment for a signal from their leader, who was holding the gun at Clint's head. And one moment was too long.

Clint grabbed at the handgun, causing it to discharge, sending a bullet to splinter the water keg and then a rivulet of water down the aisle. Courtney, ankle-deep in water, was aware of a struggle in the rear; but her eyes were riveted on Clint, who had pinned the man against the wall.

For Courtney, time stood still. Her knees turned to glue and there was a band of iron around her heart. She fought the fear. This was no time to think of herself. She must help Clint . . . check on Mrs. Rueben . . . see if other passengers were in need . . .

Outside there was the whine of a shot. But inside, the door burst open behind Clint; and the conductor, face blackened and striped cap askew, raised a shotgun.

"Git goin', ye varmints!" Without taking time for a verbal warning, he shot above the heads of all aboard.

In back of her the "varmints" were finding it hard to obey orders. They lay beneath piles of passengers who were poking, pounding, and kicking at their victims. Courtney cast only one glance back, and that quick look told her what she needed to know. Mrs.

Rueben was safe! But the men beneath the mass of furious human beings were not. How on earth had Mrs. Rueben found life enough to stand above them, spouting nonstop German and holding knitting needles dangerously close to one would-be bandit's eyes?

"Let them go, friends!" At Clint's orders, Courtney's head jerked back to him. "You are very brave—all of you—but we must not demand an eye for an eye."

Courtney's vision had cleared somewhat, and on the floor she saw pocketbooks, gold watches . . . loose change . . . a diamond stickpin . . . brooches . . . and yes, there was Mrs. Rueben's cross. But where was her own locket, the one which the insulting man had so gloated over when he forced her to surrender it? Well, he was not gloating now. He had the face of a coward—alone and at the mercy of Clint and the conductor, the bandits in back having been released and departed with the ones who had remained outside.

The echo of the escaping horses' hoofbeats died away. There was complete silence in the coach. Yet Clint's voice was so low that Courtney was sure only she heard. "Get out of here before I jerk that filthy mask from your filthier face. If the others recognized you, there would be nothing I could do to save your hide—not that you deserve it!"

So Clint recognized the man? And yet let him go? Her admiration for him grew more with his every movement. Here, surely, was a man who put mercy above justice. A part of his faith . . .

But the dizziness was back. Courtney gave a little gasp as the floor beneath her twirled the bandit's loot round and round. Clint caught her just before she fell.

His arms were iron bands, and yet they were gentle. She had not felt so safe, even in the midst of all this, since she lost her father. She swallowed hard, hoping the dryness would go away and she could thank him. But he was staring down into her face with the strangest expression—one she was unable to identify. And then the moment was gone. The corners of his mouth lifted in the beginning of a smile, and his words—when he spoke—went with it.

"Oh, Courtney, I never knew—I never dreamed—anyone so unaccustomed to the frontier could be so courageous. That was a brave thing, but—" Clint hesitated, then gave her a playful little shake, "It was very foolish! You could have been killed—"

"You could have, too!"

Clint inhaled deeply as if to calm an inner storm. "Has anyone ever told you how wonderful you are?"

Courtney dropped her eyes shyly, unaware that there was a watchful and smiling audience. "No," she said truthfully, "nobody ever has."

CHAPTER 9
The Glory Train

Methodically, one by one, passengers returned to their seats. Courtney marveled at their calm, each moving as if the whole thing had been rehearsed. In a way this was true, she supposed. These people had been through so many hardships that some invisible string held them together in any crisis. Quietly she too sat down on the hard benchseat that she and Clint had shared.

Across from her, Mrs. Rueben was stirring the stale air around her with her hankie. She had made no effort to recover her necklace. Neither had her fellow passengers. Instead, a dapper little man—his remaining black strands of hair combed forward to cover the balding forehead—rose, flicked a fluff of lint from his striped suit, and loosened his high, starched collar before moving from the middle of the coach to the front, where Clint was still talking in low tones with the engineer.

Courtney heard a murmur of approval. A drummer, they said.

As such, he was the self-appointed custodian of the treasures scattered on the soggy green strip of carpet that ran the length of the car. Picking it all up with a flourish, he held each piece up as if to auction it. But the owners knew the procedure. Each raised a hand when a possession was spied.

"Thank ye, good brother!" The big man, still clutching his Bible, boomed. Then, with frocktails flying, he hurried forward to pump the drummer's hand.

Quickly his plump fingers opened the well-worn Bible. " 'Answer not a fool according to his folly, lest thou also be like him,' " he read. "Says so right here in me book o' Proverbs. Them boogers be lik'n t'clouds 'n wind without rain—'n we be lik'n th' north wind that be drivin' 'em away!"

"Amen, amen!" The other passengers chorused.

"Now, if th' good conductor here'll be openin' some o'these bloomin' windows we be lettin' out some song—forthwith!"

"Get on board, little children," the man, obviously a preacher, sang out—his florid face becoming frighteningly red and the veins along his heavy neck swelling enormously.

And then the entire group was singing. Courtney, who had never heard the song (and Mother said that, unlike Vanessa, she had no voice), was singing too:

> Get on board, little children, get on board;
> We're on the Glory Train, little children,
> Heading for Glo-ry Land . . .

As she sang, Courtney felt an unidentifiable burden lifted from her heart. What was it in her past that had provoked such powerful feeling, puzzled confusion, anger, primal fear, sense of fragility, and—yes—uselessness of life?

The world had threatened to crumble around these people, the sense of danger lurking—threatening to end their lives, bringing pain and helplessness. Yet they sang together once the crisis was past. How . . .?

Together. That was the word. They had togetherness and they expressed their triumph over evil. It was the release she had needed when she lost her father. She needed to cry, to laugh, to sing—*anything* that would link her heart with others. Instead, she had been forced to stop fidgeting as she sat between Nanny and Mother at the funeral. Mother in that hateful veil . . . behind which there were no tears . . .

But Courtney did recall that the minister, the gray-haired man in a somber robe, understood. "The real purpose of this ritual is not only to honor the departed," he said. "It is to reestablish a common love, a release of grief, and then a sense of victory over the grave . . ."

Tears were streaming down Courtney's cheeks. The sense of release had come. It was too late to undo the eight years of isolation, but not too late to start anew. It was never too late.

She was still singing when Clint slipped into the seat beside her and took her hand. He understood too. Without words, he understood. How glorious! A common bond of joy . . .

CHAPTER 10

A New Concern

The train no longer sounded like a giant monster wearing iron shoes. In her state of exhaustion, Courtney's ears heard in the wheels a lullaby. She drifted off to sleep thinking that she and Clint had come to know each other better in this short time together than some people did in a lifetime.

Suddenly she was awake. Clint was shaking her arm gently and the train was slowing to a near-stop.

"Trouble again?" she whispered, forcing herself to stay calm.

Clint's laugh was low and pleasant. "No trouble. Good news. We're almost there. The ground's level—see?"

The forest had disappeared. On both sides of the Columbia Courtney saw a grassy plain which extended to another river that apparently flowed into the Columbia. Westward were shadowy forests. Eastward were hills that climbed higher and higher to join what Efraim's map had shown as the Cascades. And, if she remembered right, somewhere to the north—in another vast expanse of coniferous forests—was Fort Vancouver.

"How beautiful!" she said to Clint. And then, as if to herself, "but I hope those two rivers meeting head-on don't portend—well, my meeting with Cousin Arabella—"

She stopped abashed at what she must have said aloud. "Cousin *Bella*," Clint corrected with a smile. "And, you need have no fear of our relative, Courtney. She's a strange one but has a lump of silver for a heart."

"*Our* relative. I feel embarrassed to ask—but I don't know how we're related. In fact—" Courtney bit her lower lip in concentration, "I'm not sure if Cousin Ara—Cousin Bella—is a Glamora or a Bellevue."

She stopped short of saying more. It would be downright forward of her to ask further about her relationship to him. But deep in her heart was a feeling of regret that they were of the same family. She must put the thought away—

Clint pretended to be horrified. "How could you?" he teased. Then, in a more serious tone, he explained. "I was serious when I told Mrs. Thorpe that I was Aunt Bella's nephew and that my mother was her half-sister. The relationship was on the father's side. Grandfather Jed had only the one daughter by Robert Glamora—"

"Then Cousin Bella is—"

Clint nodded. "—of the Glamora clan," he finished.

"I should have known by the fact that she came to my father's funeral."

"No," Clint said slowly, "no, you would have had no way of knowing. You were very young—and there were other matters that needed settling."

What matters, Clint? Tell me. Maybe they will give

me the key to why I am here!

But Clint was pointing at a freshly cleared and plowed field—obviously rich and productive even to Courtney's untrained eye. "Grandpa Jed used to say that the virgin soil, when freshly turned, looked good enough for dessert!"

Courtney looked at the chocolate-colored earth. And how much a part of it Clint was, this beautiful man who fitted in so perfectly with the wild beauty of the land. And who, praise be, was not her cousin!

With the thought, she turned a radiant smile on him.

"That's a beautiful smile—and at a stranger! You don't know my identity yet!"

I don't care! Courtney's heart cried out. But she managed a tremulous, "Tell me."

Clint chuckled. "My mother, for better or worse, managed to get herself three husbands. I am a bit prejudiced, I guess, but I happen to think my father was the best of the lot. And I have a strong ally. You see, the other two were of the Bellevue clan—two sons by each."

Courtney caught her breath. "So they—the four men—are my cousins—not you. Do they—are they friendly?"

The train gave a shrill whistle, drowning out any answer Clint may have made. "We're here!" he said, but she read concern in his eyes.

CHAPTER 11
Strange Reunion

It was good to stand on solid ground again. And so good to breathe in the clean, sweet air. The train, having shuddered to a stop, was quiet. And in the silence Courtney heard the babbling of a busy stream. Following the sound with her eyes, she saw where it emptied into the Columbia near what must be Fort Vancouver, as there was so much activity. And beyond she spotted a busy gristmill and, yes, surely that was a lumbermill. Farther out lay miles of cultivated fields and orchards, divided by meadows and pastures grazed over by thousands of cattle and sheep.

And there! The little island where the two rivers met . . . what did Efraim's map call the one entering the Columbia? Willamette? But in her mind was another name—something Clint had said about a mysterious person called Donolar, who referred to his part of the world as "Innisfree."

"Hard to believe that Portland had only two

painted houses, one brick one, a few cabins, and three frame buildings, not painted, just a generation ago. Now there are mills, 18 stores and a line of ships lying along the waterfront. They're what caught the imaginative eye of Grandpa Jed—"

Clint paused to shift the load of baggage, giving Courtney the opportunity to glance in the opposite direction.

"I was too enthralled with the scenery," she admitted, glancing around to check on the whereabouts of Mrs. Rueben. "Why did your grandfather care about the port?"

"Shipping—his father before him had discovered the mineral-rich territory northeast of the Columbia."

And southwest of the river, she supposed, was Portland. Courtney craned her neck, felt a stab of pain from sitting in the cramped position for so long, and gave up, carrying with her the impression of busy streets, still unpaved, running wildly in every direction like rabbits trying to escape a briarpatch. Roads, wide as fields, surrounded a vast huddle of weathered buildings. There had been no time to read any of the signs except the one marked HOSTELRY. Would they have to spend the night here? Courtney shivered, hoping not.

For one moment the old childhood fears came back—the ones she had thought buried. Alone in her grief, Courtney remembered shutting her eyes tightly against the shadows, trembling uncontrollably at the rumble of thunder, and jumping when someone called her name. What was she doing out here alone, anyway? Facing a strange world was courting disaster. Involuntarily she reached for Clint's hand. And at that moment Mrs. Rueben joined them, cupping her hand to her ear and straining eastward.

A buggy of ancient vintage was crossing a bridge over the small stream. Every board clattered in announcement of the arrival of the erect woman and the pale-faced youth beside her.

Courtney had worried unnecessarily about not recognizing her cousin. She was relieved when she remembered Arabella Kennedy at once. It was the same authoritative figure, and Courtney wondered how she could have failed to recognize her father's "dark side" in his kin. She was tall and somewhat angular, but in possession of a certain compelling charm that Courtney observed as the youth beside her helped her from the buggy—a certain regal air even in the simple black-and-white attire. Maybe that was what enhanced it, Courtney thought, as her heavy black braids—once she removed the black bonnet—were streaked with white.

Was she staring? She must have been, Courtney realized, for Clint gave her arm a little squeeze as if reminding her to step forward in greeting.

Not sure of what was called for, Courtney lowered her eyes demurely and curtsied.

"Ah, my dear Courtney, how charming! Are you famished—or shall we try and outrun the darkness to the mansion?"

Something in her voice told Courtney that an answer was not called for. She was right. "But, of course, you will wish to freshen up. I must say, the three of you look like chimney sweeps!"

Arabella Kennedy did not smile, but her voice was deep, rich, and low—reminding Courtney of Clint's. As Clint, Mrs. Rueben (who seemed to understand),

and the strange young man laughed, Cousin Bella moved closer to Courtney.

She laid a slender hand on Courtney's shoulder, and for a moment Courtney wondered if there was to be an embrace.

Apparently not. Instead, the woman was studying her closely. "Like your father, and that's good," she said with a cutting edge to her voice. "Of course, I knew that all along—yes, you'll do!"

"Thank you," Courtney said softly, wondering what she was thanking her cousin for.

Wondering who the lad who had driven Cousin Bella to meet them could be, Courtney cast a look his direction. He was very young, she judged, and very friendly. At least, there was a smile on his lips. But his eyes—so wide, innocent, and agate-colored—had no expression at all. His pale thatch of hair, curling childishly at the neckline, made him look even more youthful. That is why Courtney was so surprised when Clint, looking over his shoulder as he loaded in the baggage, introduced the boy.

"This is Donolar," he said.

Donolar! This child who quoted from Yeats' writing?

"How do you do, Donolar?" Courtney said politely. "I understand that you enjoy literature—surprising for one so young—"

"Donolar helps us keep the mansion going. He is past the age of schooling. Shall we go?" Cousin Bella interrupted.

Something about the boy—or was he a man?—both puzzled and fascinated Courtney. She found herself strangely drawn to the innocent face—while fearing it. She would ask Clint.

"I will show you the butterflies and the bees. They

are my friends, and 'where the bee sucks there suck I.' "

Shakespeare! Suddenly the carriage was moving northeast toward Washington . . . the mines . . . the mansion. And Innisfree!

CHAPTER 12

Mansion-in-the-Wild

The sunset was spectacular. Cousin Bella occupied the front seat of the rig, beside the driver which put the housekeeper, Courtney, and Clint in the back. Mrs. Rueben made no effort to separate the two this time.

They turned in a grove of firs, massed together so heavily with wild-grape vines that Courtney thought surely they would have to hack their way through. But somebody had done it before them, and something resembling a road twisted and turned through the green maze until Courtney lost all sense of direction.

Wordlessly, lest he frighten the animals, Clint pointed out plump rabbits, skinny-legged coyotes, and a speckled fawn. An animal's paradise. But *people* lived here?

Apparently they did, because twice during the long, rough ride he pointed out thin plumes of smoke rising from fat chimneys of small cabins of unpeeled logs. Courtney, enchanted by the surroundings and frightened at the same time, was grateful for the rifle—or was it a musket?—that lay at Clint's feet. In fact, she was grateful for Clint's nearness, an emotion she dared not examine too closely . . .

Suddenly the world spun out of focus. With a little moan she covered her hair with her bare hands.

"What is it?" Clint, warned by her low cry, whispered as he reached for the gun.

Courtney's throat was dust-dry and beyond sound. Lifting one hand momentarily from her head, she managed to point to where she had seen the nut-brown body, clad only in a loincloth of animal skin—and surely those were scalps dangling from the bottom. Oh, the horror of the painted face—red, slashed with white, and wearing a plume of eagle feathers. Now another had joined him. The woods were undoubtedly full of these savages! Courtney, forgetting her scalp, clasped her hands over her mouth to silence the scream that had overcome the dryness.

"It's all right, my darling—it's all right," Clint soothed as he bent to put the gun back in its place. "The only Indians you're apt to see hereabouts are either on their way to trade their pelts for food at Fort Vancouver or those who, like our present spectators, look at us out of curiosity."

"They never cause trouble?" Courtney was still trembling, which was probably why Clint put a supporting arm across her shoulders.

"Oh, there are a few who are still hostile. But even they become less so if one carries a few trinkets. We have more problems with tribes warring among themselves—and—" Clint hesitated, "it shames me to say white men's attacks on their red brothers."

"You don't see them as savages? Men who carry tomahawks and steal white women's locks—maybe the women themselves?"

Clint laughed softly. Then, patting her shoulder gently, he said, "Courtney, it is the white men you must watch out for."

She missed the warning in his voice. "That's a relief in one way and a shame in another. What a disappointment for Efraim!"

"Efraim?"

"My brother," Courtney said. And then she was telling him all about Efraim's dreams . . . Vanessa's beauty and talent . . . and, before she realized it, the old Bellevue-Glamora feud and how it had affected her immediate family so directly.

"It makes me sad," she said slowly as if talking to herself, "knowing somehow that I will never see Waverly Manor again. I don't know for sure why Mother wanted me here. She has sent me away many times—after I lost my father—"

"Something tells me you were a lonely little girl—more lonely in a crowd than in a so-called lonely country."

"Something tells me you may be right," Courtney said. "And, oh, Efraim's coming one day—and there's Lance—"

"Lance? What is he to you?"

"I—I'm not really sure," Courtney said truthfully.

The forest parted, allowing Courtney to look ahead at the chain of mountains rising to meet the sunset sky, creating an impregnable fortress around the valleys below. Twilight was wrapping a soft purple shawl around their granite peaks now capped with snow. Powerfully, those towering peaks pushed the clouds aside to leave Courtney wondering if they pierced the sky in an effort to be the floor of heaven. Oh, the beauty of it all!

Courtney leaned her head on Clint's shoulder, lifting her face to watch as twilight's blue turned to black and one by one the stars came out like sequins strung on black velvet.

Somewhere there was the hoot of an owl, followed by the lonely cry of a coyote. Then the woods were filled with a din of night creatures hooting, howling, and shrieking. Frightening? Ordinarily . . . but, exhausted, Courtney slept.

Courtney was only dimly aware when the buggy made a turn into what must be a driveway of sorts. "Grandest house hereabouts," Clint told her from a million miles away. "Mansion-in-the-Wild."

A few minutes later she was soaking in a tub of lavender-scented water that Cousin Bella ordered brought to her room . . . relaxing . . . letting every muscle unwind . . . hardly aware of her surroundings, except that they were vast. Vast. Dark. And very much out of place in this strange, new land.

What must have been hours later, she awakened slowly—dazed and wondering where she was. Somewhere there was the hum of voices which came closer and closer. Clint and Cousin Bella.

"And you know for sure who the robbers were—but of course you do!" Cousin Bella's voice was bitter.

"Yes, Aunt Bella, I know—but for now, it's our secret—"

The voices drifted away.

CHAPTER 13
Strange New Ways

Courtney looked around her in dismay. It was such a strange room. The beamed ceiling seemed to be reaching for light. Small wonder, with the long, narrow windows covered with heavy drapes that defied any intrusion of the gloom. The furniture, old but rubbed to a soft sheen, was heavy with marble supported by claw feet. The effort was one of heaviness, gloom, and darkness . . . so oppressive that it was hard to breathe.

Somehow she knew that the outside of the mansion would be somewhat the same—hard to describe but outrageously out of place . . . lonely . . . misplaced . . . and pompous in its attempt at grandiosity.

Courtney was examining the canopy bed in which she had spent the night when she heard singing, faint at first and then drawing closer. One did not associate such melodious sounds with either Cousin Bella or Mrs. Rueben. She strained to hear.

"Swing low, sweet char-i-ot, comin' fo' t'carry me home . . ."

The voice trailed off and there was a soft knock. "Miz Courtney?" The door opened and there stood a massive black woman with a wide, pearly-toothed smile that dared the world to try and dull her sunny disposition. "Miz Arabella's ordered breakfast for th' two y'all. Ah brung it. Ah'm Mandy."

"Thank you, Mandy," Courtney said, liking her at once.

"Yes, thank you, Mandy. I'll take the tray," Cousin Bella said, entering behind the cook.

As soon as the massive door swung shut, Cousin Bella drew a chair up beside the bed without words. Courtney felt awkward in her relative's presence and a bit apprehensive.

"Do I intimidate you, my dear?" Cousin Bella asked in greeting.

"No—I—it's all so strange and new—"

Arabella Kennedy poured two cups of coffee, handing one to Courtney without appearing to bend her back.

"Are you afraid here?"

Courtney accepted sugar and cream, stirring the coffee slowly before speaking. "In a way that I can't explain."

"Thank you for being honest, Courtney. You are a Glamora all right! You will find me—how shall I say it?—undemonstrative. I never had a family, you know, so I will have as much to learn from you as you from me. Just because I seem withdrawn does not mean that I do not care."

"I understand, Cousin Bella. I am so often tongue-tied."

"You and I are going to make quite a team," Cousin Bella said with approval. "Would you like to try Mandy's famous sourdough biscuits? We cure our hams, too."

Courtney looked at the proffered platter. "I prefer seeing what I eat—unless light is forbidden."

Cousin Bella laughed for the first time. "That is why I sent for you—to add some light to this place. I was only too happy to honor your mother's request—"

Her voice was lost behind the heavy drapes—an advantage, Courtney guessed. At any rate, it was taking a long time to push back the thick damask and let sunlight flood the room.

Arabella Kennedy was clearly an honest, open woman, though maybe a bit blunt. Courtney felt that her cousin would appreciate the same qualities in other people as well.

"Why did she send me away? Mother *asked* you to invite me here?"

"She told you nothing? No, I can see that she did not. How like her! But I welcomed the chance to have a legitimate excuse. You see, I have planned this for a long, long time . . . but it is too soon to go into that. Let's cross one bridge at a time. You know that there is no love lost between your father's side and your mother's. You are a bright little girl—always were—*too* bright to suit Cousin Gabriel's Lady Ana!"

Courtney, to her surprise, found herself enjoying the conversation, as well as the meal. She bit into a yeasty biscuit, made even more palatable with extravagant spreadings of butter and honey.

"I am not the bright one," Courtney blurted before

realizing her mouth was too full. Self-consciously she swallowed, then went on, "Efraim's brilliant and Vanessa's beautiful."

" 'Still water runs deep,' but that too is another story. Suffice it to say that I have three reasons for wanting you here, all of them important and one *especially* so. But first things first: I *do* want and need a companion. But we shall not rush into that either. First, I want you to see the entire estate and the mines. Showing you around will be Clint's job. Incidentally, my dear, how was your trip?"

"Tedious," Courtney admitted, "until I met Clint—Clint and Mrs. Rueben, that is," she amended self-consciously.

Cousin Bella gave her another look of approval. "I am glad you two got along so well," she said matter-of-factly, ignoring mention of the housekeeper's name.

"I have an immense collection of books. Clint and Donolar both make use of the library. You see, I do not want you to be lonely or homesick—or considering going back, ever."

Courtney blotted her mouth with the white linen napkin on her tray, then wet her lips. "Are you going to tell me why—"

"Not until after grace."

Grace! Why, they had eaten already. And the few times that there was grace at the table after her father's death Courtney could count on the fingers on one hand. Just a ritualistic overture.

Cousin Bella looked amused. "Maybe the Lord appreciates a *thank you* after a meal more than before! You do the honors."

Courtney remembered but one prayer. Obediently she lowered her head: "God is great; God is good;

and we thank Him for this food."

Cousin Bella inhaled deeply. "That'll do for starters. But do you realize you talked *about* our Provider, not *to* Him?"

There was so much to learn. . .

CHAPTER 14

The Dinner Hour

The first day at the Mansion-in-the-Wild, and the week to follow, were so full that Courtney found no time for homesickness. Of all the surprises in this new land, that was the one which perplexed her most. But her busy schedule left her no time to think on that either, even of the letters to write.

Cousin Bella let it be known from the first day that dinner was served promptly at six o'clock and that all were expected to be on time. Courtney was unaware who the "all" included until her ride with Clint. That too was arranged by Arabella Kennedy.

"You do have riding clothes?"

"Yes, I rode back home—never in proper attire—"

"All the better! Now, get dressed. Clint is waiting with his horse and a tame little mare you will enjoy."

Courtney did not see Clint at first. Once outside, she was too busy exploring the enormous house in which she was a guest. The upper windows reflected the morning sun through swaying fir boughs, returning the molten-gold of the mirrored light to finger in the flowering fruit trees that lined the drive. There was a lush vegetable garden at the back of the house, and beyond was a rose garden that came from a storybook. Just where the carefully pruned bushes ended, the ground sloped downward to a shimmering stream. And around it all were the eternal mountains, some cloaked in the green of vast forests, others made pink by the early sunrays on the snow. And everywhere there were meadows, scalloped in flowers. . . so lovely for Lance to paint someday. But for now her eyes were drawn back to the ancient house that surely some mad architect must have designed!

The great house seemed to ramble, bulge, and loom up in unexpected places as if in a game of hide-and-seek. Courtney found herself spellbound, wondering how the strange house came to its present shape. As little as she knew about architecture, she was sure that a part of Mansion-in-the-Wild was as old as the civilization of the area itself. But there were strange additions to the early architecture. It was grotesque—"Castle Ugly" she would call it to Lance—and yet there was something appealing about it. It was like a house one might stumble upon in the dark forests of a fairy tale. . . a house that had enlarged to accommodate a growing family, making room for every pilgrim in need. . . watched over by some beneficent fairy godmother—not necessarily versed in the arts, but with an enormous heart. . .

"Strange, isn't it?" Courtney did not jump, although Clint's voice was unexpected. He was simply a natural part of the setting. "Legend has it that the house began as a home for Dr. McLoughlin.

The fence," Clint made a circle of immense diameter to show logs planed by the passage of time surrounding the innumerable buildings behind the main house, "served as a barrier from danger."

Clint dismounted and made ready to help Courtney astride the little mare. But not now! Not with so much to learn.

"What was he, this Dr. McLoughlin, to us?"

Clint looked at her appreciatively. "How good to find someone in addition to Aunt Bella and me who cares! The great man, so important in the Columbia Country's history, was—would you believe?—a distant relative of the Glamoras. That is why the family so wanted what was left of the massive house after the death of Dr. McLoughlin and his widow. That's what was left—see the adobe-like brick foundation on the east wing?"

Courtney could only nod. She was fascinated with the history. And she was very much aware that Clint was running his fingers through her hair as he pushed it from her face.

"It's good that this was almost two generations ago! What a beautiful trophy this black cloud of hair would have made!"

Courtney heard him give a little gasp of admiration as her hair, hurriedly pinned up to go beneath her felt hat, fell into a soft black cloud almost to her waist. For one moment she closed her eyes, yielding to the healing touch of his hand. Her head still ached from the long journey. It was comforting to have his fingers touch the muscles so stiff and sore with tension. This was better than a headache powder. But it was certainly improper. Come to think of it, it was improper to be riding with a man unchaperoned. Strange that Aunt Bella would have initiated such a situation.

"Clint—we must go—remember the warning about the dinner hour?"

Automatically her eyes looked anxiously to the upstairs windows. And, sure enough, the curtains, parted for a fleeting second, closed. But not before Courtney saw her cousin's face. She—why, she looked actually pleased with herself.

Clint laughed as he helped her onto the mare. "Aunt Bella is very pleased with you and admires you greatly. Comfortable?"

"Yes, thank you." Courtney said primly, but hoping that Clint would keep talking. She was unsure which she wanted more to hear—the history which might hold some clue as to her presence here, or Clint's compliments. She felt her cheeks grow warm with embarrassment at her vanity.

"Aunt Bella has a marvelous library. We'll explore it together—the books, the old diaries. And what we don't know Donolar will tell us!" Clint said without meeting her eyes.

Courtney wanted to know more about the boy, too. But, before she had a chance to phrase a question, Clint had changed the subject. Flattery she must never allow, Nanny had warned. And here she was allowing it. Inviting it. *Willing* it!

Clint tightened the reins, a signal for his horse to head toward the rose garden and the little stream. "Let's go, girls," he said to the ponies. Then, as they moved slowly toward the loveliness ahead, Clint said, "Oh, I must tell you what my conversative aunt said. Unbelievable! I overheard her tell Mandy and Mrs. Rueben that only a real beauty could wear her hair with a smooth center-part, but that it was right for you because of your oval face—'angelic' she called it!"

Courtney's heart picked up speed. She dared listen to no more of this. She gave the mare's ribs a gentle touch with her heels, and immediately the mare and the rider were ahead.

"Not fair!" Clint called from behind, laughter in his voice. At his words the rose bushes parted as if pushed aside by an unseen hand. And there, to her surprise, was a small, well-built log cabin. For a moment she was startled. A boy had parted the shrubs and was standing directly in her path. Donolar!

Courtney felt a strong desire to rein in and talk with the boy. But there was no time. The childish—yet wondrously wise—face was gone. And Clint's pony was beside her as if the rider had urged her forward to deter any conversation.

The rose garden was beautifully laid out, reminding Courtney of the carefully landscaped grounds done by skillful gardeners of the "well-to-do." Nobody back home bothered following the winding trails to enjoy nature. Gardens yielded cut flowers for formal bouquets—and, as Mother said, it was the thing to do, having a garden.

But here it was different—people cared. Just look at the beds of dewy roses against the natural wilderness of the surrounding terrain! And now, suddenly, they had come to a rustic little log bridge that set the sunbeams dancing in the ripples of the stream. Here beauty was meant to be enjoyed.

"I'll go first to show you it's safe," Clint smiled.

Courtney gave him a little affirmative salute. Actually, no thought of danger had crossed her mind. But, once they were on the other side, Clint waited for her to join him.

"Aunt Bella has appointed me, without your vote or mine, as your guardian." Clint spoke lightly, but something in his thoughtful blue eyes put meaning behind the words. "I don't want you to be afraid, but I don't want you doing foolhardy things like you did in that train, young lady—proud of you though I was."

"I will be careful," Courtney promised, partly from her pattern of obedience and, admittedly, partly because the woods they were approaching were shadow-filled along the edges. Then, as if in warning, the shadows blended into one. Bears, wolves, *Indians*? No, Clint had said they were friendly—not that she cared to get too close.

Courtney was startled out of her preoccupation with her own questions by Clint's posing one of his own. "Like it?"

"It's beautiful," she murmured. "I can see why you named it 'Dream Country.' " Then, looking back over her shoulder, she added, "and I understand Donolar's name. His rose garden is truly an island in the wilderness . . . 'Isle of Innisfree' . . ."

They had come to a little rise, and in the distance Courtney could see a few slender plumes of smoke rising to meet the morning sun. Cabins? Surely there were closer neighbors. There was time to find out. Now she wanted to know more about the strange young man who had created a fantasy land.

"Tell me about Donolar, Clint."

Did she imagine he hesitated before telling her that Donolar was trustworthy, good, and kind? He possessed a special gift of communicating with plants and animals, Clint explained.

"But not mankind?" Courtney guessed.

"It depends on the person, the time, and the place, and something else I am unable to define. He is withdrawn—sometimes straining toward genius and sometimes, well, highly imaginative—"

"How long has he been here? And," she asked, remembering the cherub face, "how old is he?"

"The story really belongs to my aunt, Courtney—and, I might add, she does not welcome questions. I will say simply that he has been here for a long, long time—coming under rather mysterious circumstances. Aunt Bella, in true tradition of the Mansion, took him in when he was only—well, very young—and, discovering his fine mind, started him reading, since school was hardly the place for a person of his highly imaginative mind. People can be cruel—children, too—even though he's grown up—"

"*How* grown up?"

"He has the mind of a child—in some ways—but his years measure 21."

"Efraim's age!" Courtney whispered in dismay.

"And just a little below mine. Come now—I'll race you to that next rise. We'll share an apple and some jerky."

This time it was Clint who nudged the mare and got the head start. "Time about's fair play!"

The apples were sweet and succulent. But jerky? Courtney doubted that it was as tasty as Clint claimed. Smoking venison over a bed of coals was not her idea of cooking. She nibbled, murmured "M-m-m-m," and took another piece. As Clint cut the strips of dried meat into bite-size chunks with his bowie knife, he suddenly chuckled.

"I find you as puzzling as Donolar. On occasion you possess all the regal dignity of a queen reigning over her court. Seconds later my queen has turned into a shy little princess to whom everything in the world is new—a sweet child—"

"Everything in this part of the world *is*—but I am not a child. I'm almost 17." Courtney had risen and was standing as tall as her petite frame would stretch.

Clint busied himself picking up the remains of their lunch. "Not a child, she says—but *sweet*. Sweet 16—"

"Seventeen!" Courtney corrected, feeling older than her years, wiser, and *almost* attractive. It was the air, that's what it was. Why, she felt actually dizzy inhaling its rarity. It was like one of those secret dreams of Courtney's—and it had come true. The scenery, beautiful before, suddenly now became awesome—almost too much to bear. Mountains stretched as far as the eye could see, divided by deep ravines and silver waterfalls that seemed to be pouring from the sky.

"You know," Clint said from so close behind her that Courtney could feel his breath lifting a strand of her hair, "only God could arrange such scenery—and such moments. Up here alone I can feel His touch—smell it in each wildflower . . . see it in the rim of the sky above those hills . . . feel it in the pine-scented breeze. I am so glad to share His moment of love with you. Hey! That race is going to be a *real* one home. Remember Aunt Bella's command—six o'clock sharp!"

• • •

The dream continued throughout the dinner hour. It was filled with surprises. The day had left Courtney with more questions than answers. And dinner created more. And, yet, in a strange sort of way, there were answers, too—the strange part being that they were answers to questions left unasked.

CHAPTER 15
The Pattern Is Set

The pattern for life in Mansion-in-the-Wild was set from the first meal together. Mandy was a great help. Dinner was " 'most ready," the cook announced, her ebony face wreathed in smiles, so would Miz Courtney be likin' somethin' that'd help out?

"Yes, I would, Mandy," Courtney said solemnly. "Your advice. I need to know what to wear."

"Well, now, Miz Arabella's sorta peculiar-like—you know, not one whit uppity—but particular-like. She takes a likin' t' black 'n white." Mandy was already looking over the line of clothes in the closet where she had hung them while Courtney explored the estate. "Oh! here 'tis!"

Mandy had selected a simple white, floor-length dress. The kimono sleeves stopped just below the elbow, a style that Mandy expected to meet with Cousin Arabella's standards. But was the neck a little low? It needed something. The stolen locket would be just right. Courtney sighed deeply, wondering if she would ever see the beloved necklace again. Not trusting her voice, Courtney smiled and turned away. Mandy seemed to take the motion as one of dismissal.

Once the woman was out of the room, Courtney reached for the red-ribbon sash. It would give the dress some life. But no, she would not wear it. Her waist needed no cinching, as it was no more than a hand-span already. And, while she had no intention of being committed to the no-color choices of her cousin, for now it was wise to conform.

But isn't there another reason, Courtney? The question seemed to come from her own reflection as she brushed her long hair into place. Startled, she laid the brush on the dresser. For a moment she stared at her reflection angrily. Angrily it stared back. Then, ever so slowly, Courtney's lips lifted at the corners with the beginning of a smile. *All right*, she answered the reflection, *so you are right! I want him to like me! The sash is too young for me.*

How foolish she was. But the discovery—or had she always known?—sent her whirling and twirling about the room. The wide sweep of her skirt stood out as if supported by a hoop, and her feet kept time to imagined music. Faster . . . faster . . . *faster*!

When a faint tinkle of the dinner bell came, Courtney hurried down the winding stairs, heart pounding and face aglow. She needed no color to make the dress come alive.

In that state of euphoria, Courtney failed to see another woman coming up the stairs until they both reached the landing marking the halfway bend. At that point the soft lights from the shaded lamps in the hall below wiped out the upper darkness. So she had to be fully visible. How then did she all but fall over the other person—unless—but, no, she dared not think that anyone would purposely block the way.

"Really, you should watch where you're going!"

"I—I'm truly very sorry—" Courtney gasped. It was hard to put words together when she was so totally embarrassed or when she found herself looking into the face of such a flaming-haired beauty. The red hair, backlighted by the lamplight, was pure gold. And there were a million candles glowing in the enormous green eyes—anger giving way to a certain civility, so that the expression was one of innocence. And, as she watched, Courtney saw the slash of a red mouth soften slightly.

But the voice was still unfriendly, even though there was exaggerated demureness in its tone. "Why, you must be the sweet child Mrs. Kennedy has taken in. She is so good about such deeds. Just look at what she's done for that pitiful piece of humanity, Donolar—you have met him?"

Color burned Courtney's face and her heart beat against her ribs with such force that she grasped the rail to keep from falling. It was the first time in her life she had been so angry, and something which had lain dormant for years begged to be released. But her good breeding forced her to breathe deeply. And, sure enough, after a few dizzy turns, her mind settled down.

Extending her hand, she said in her normal voice, "I am Courtney Glamora, Miss Kennedy's cousin. I don't believe you and I have met."

The girl's laugh was an insult, gay but mocking. Her voice was pitched low, giving Courtney the distinct suspicion that she welcomed no other audience.

"No, we have not met! But I have met some of your relatives!"

There was a hidden meaning behind the words, but Courtney chose to ignore it. "At this point, you have the advantage then. You have not told me your name."

"Oh, my dear, I would have supposed Clint told you. We have been sweethearts for so long I suppose he thinks even the—the newcomers know. He has not told you of Alexis Worthington?"

So that was it. Alexis Worthington, whoever she was, was jealous. Courtney made a sudden decision not to give this insulting young lady the satisfaction of knowing there was nothing between her and Clint. She remained quiet and was pleased that a flicker of envy crossed the haughty face. Alexis had known of her presence. Well, what had she expected? A pig-faced simpleton?

Alexis had regained her poise. "Well, I doubt that you will wish to stay long. You'll starve in this wilderness."

"If I starve in this wilderness it will be from no lack of food, companionship—or love!"

Alexis Worthington's lips turned white with anger. Gathering a fur-trimmed cape about her, she started up the stairs, head held high.

"I left my gloves in Clint's room. As I am sure you know, he stays with his aunt when he is not at the mines. He and I were there today—so much to catch up on, you know. Well, I do believe your dinner is waiting."

With a low, insinuating laugh, she turned away. But not before Courtney called after her, "There is a lot I do not know, Miss Worthington—and a lot you do not know either. I am not a child. Donolar is not an idiot. And, no, Clint has not mentioned your name!"

Lifting her skirts, Courtney hurried down the remaining stairs. Alexis Worthington had fired the first shot. Let her win the war!

What was happening to her anyway? Was the new land changing her already? Good breeding forbade her speaking to anyone as she had spoken to "Clint's sweetheart"! But, then, she had never had anyone refuse her proffered hand before . . . and, yes, she was as jealous as this lady with the flaming hair!

• • •

Arabella Kennedy, in a heavy black taffeta dress that swished with each breath, was seated at the end of a long table set for eight when Courtney entered the dining room. Her first impression was one of black and white again, the starched whiteness of the linen cloth sweeping to the floor to fold around the pleats of the hostess's skirts.

But the starkness was broken by an enormous bouquet of magnificent roses as a centerpiece. What a beautiful still-life subject that would make for Lance's brushes—each petal so perfect, and each blossom so unlike its neighbor! Full-blown yellow roses. Fat red rosebuds poutingly opening one or two petals. And wee pink rosebuds clenched like baby-fists.

Courtney, feeling lightheaded from the heavy aroma, moved toward the arrangement in fascination. It was as if the roses were speaking, had a message for her.

Suddenly aware that others were entering the room, Courtney whispered an apology to her cousin.

"I—I'm sorry—it's just that I was so intrigued by the roses—"

Cousin Bella nodded. "It pleases me that you noticed. They're from Innisfree. Donolar cares for them and arranges our bouquets according to his—well, the mood of the day."

Courtney did not understand, but there was no time to ask. Cousin Bella was instructing Clint to seat Courtney between himself and Donolar. The others would occupy their usual places, she said.

Courtney was a spectator, having no part in the scene around her. It was more like a stage play than real life. It was so formal, yet so informal—Clint and Donolar seating themselves and then Arabella Kennedy ringing the tiny silver bell. At the sound Mandy appeared with a platter of trout, fresh mustard greens, several unidentifiable dishes, and an enormous tray of freshly baked bread. Mrs. Rueben came in and lighted the candles at each end of the roses. Then both women sat down at the table!

"We are all one family here," Cousin Bella said to nobody in particular. "And, as such, we pray together."

She reached both hands out in signal. And in response Clint took his aunt's hand and then lifted Courtney's right just as Donolar took her left. It was a family circle where all were equal. Somehow she knew that any one of them would add "in the eyes of God."

But it was a peculiar circle, strangely askew at the end opposite the hostess as Mandy and Mrs. Rueben reached across the empty chair to clasp hands. Courtney hoped the Lord would forgive her, but wasn't the eldest male supposed to serve as host when there was no man-of-the-house?

Donolar's great agate eyes caught and held her gaze. Innocently, in that moment of reverence, he said in a low voice, "The chair's for *him*—"

Cousin Bella cleared her throat. And, like two guilty children, Donolar and Courtney bowed their heads. *It is all right*, Clint's powerful, warm hand over hers reassured her. And then he prayed.

At first Courtney listened only to the deep intonation of Clint's voice. It was a beautiful ritual. Then, suddenly, it was not a ritual at all! He had spoken her name! It was hard for her—like the rest of the people here—to face the unknown, but hearts could bring God into every situation, he said.

There was something that Courtney was unable to understand taking place inside her. It was as if this great love that Clint acknowledged flowed downward like a Washington waterfall—dropping joyfully downward to Clint and channeling from his heart to hers. Unconsciously she gripped his hand tighter as she listened to his prayer for all at the table and for someone he called "Doc George."

The prayer may have lasted only a minute, but Courtney felt that it spanned a lifetime. This was a moment she must not let go. God loves us, Clint said. God cares about us. "And You want us to be happy!" he ended.

Is it true, Your Lordship? Courtney's heart asked silently, *even for us who have not been introduced?*

"All you have to do is ask!"

Where did the words come from? Who spoke them? At first, questions crowded into Courtney's heart. And then there was a sweet peace that wiped away all doubts. It made no difference. Love's soft whisper had come. And her life would never be the same again. . .love would be her constant companion. . .

"Well!" Cousin Bella's commanding expletive broke a silence that had fallen since the chorus of *Amens*. "Are you two going to hold hands all evening, or shall we ask Mandy to serve!"

Courtney let go of Clint's hand as though it had burned her, causing a round of good-natured laughter. Even as Courtney felt a hot flush wash her face, she felt the love around her.

It was Donolar who spoke first. "The two of them should hold hands even as we dine. 'The flowers in silence seem to breathe such thoughts as language cannot tell,' Sir Tom Moore told us. So, I ask you to look at the thornless roses which tell of early attachment born of friendship!"

Courtney was deeply touched. Aware that her cheeks were still aflame but sure that her eyes were brilliant, she said shyly, "Your roses are beautiful, Donolar—just beautiful."

"More beautiful tonight because they know you admire them. Roses know. They know many secrets. Sometimes they tell the butterflies and they tell me—"

"Donolar! Lean back a bit so Mandy can serve you—"

Cousin Bella's order brought obedience. But, even as Donolar drew his chest in, he continued talking. "Now, the yellow roses are different. They tell of the decrease of love. She was here today—I saw her, meddling around in the library upstairs. And so pleased with herself. Well, the roses know! 'The contented rose is one whose blossoms are about to fall'—"

Cousin Bella put down her fork. "Do you mean she was here after my making it known she was unwelcome? How dare Alexis Villard!"

Villard? But she had called herself Alexis Worthington. Courtney glanced at Clint and saw that his face was ashen.

Mandy brought in an enormous apple cobbler. As she served, Arabella regained her composure. "Have you a picture of Gabe—your father—dear?" She asked Courtney.

"The bandits took it," Courtney said.

CHAPTER 16

A Moment of Love

Home seemed far, far away. Which it was, Courtney reflected, as she dressed for a visit to the mines the next day. The distance she felt was more than a matter of miles; it was a state of mind. Although hemmed in by mountain locks, she was enjoying a new freedom, as if the towering mountains were a fortress to keep others out instead of holding her prisoner. And she was reveling in all of it in a way she did not understand. Lonely? Not at all. Not with all these wonderful people surrounding her—and Clint. Especially Clint. Then, there was something else—something greater than the both of them. Love.

Only one thing troubled her—the unanswered questions, the mysteries, each somehow folding in as an intricate part of some giant pattern. And there were so many questions looming one after the other that Courtney realized guiltily she had all but forgotten her family . . . even the tormenting question as to why Mother had sent her away . . .

On this morning's ride, Clint took Courtney in the opposite direction—a way that led through a deep forest with trees so tall they swept the sky. She was speechless with awe. It was a sacred moment. And Clint must have known.

He reined in beside a small stream. Courtney stopped too, and Clint helped her down and planted her feet on the busy stream's mossy bank. Except for the chatting of the brook, there was total silence.

"It's like a cathedral," Clint said in the low tone reserved for hallowed ground.

Courtney, her heart full, nodded.

"Do you feel His presence here with us?"

"I feel His presence with me everywhere now. Oh, Clint, if God had an earthly home, this would be it."

"Oh, my darling, God is here—here in our hearts."

There! Clint had used that term of endearment again. Courtney found herself trembling. Did hearts ever burst from love? *Earthly love. . . heavenly love. . . love that released, forgave, healed?* The pine trees whispered softly of its power.

"Oh, little Courtney, how like a little Madonna angel you look. Would that the world were as sweet, as innocent, as able to spread happiness—"

Clint took the one step that lay between them and, taking her hands in his, drew her to him. He rested his chin on her bare head. Their bodies did not touch.

Of course not, she thought sadly. He was a man—a mature man whose presence stirred her—not a boy like Lance. But his words, loving though they were, confused her. Did he look upon her as an amusing child? One who could spread happiness, he had said. And she, well, what *had* she done? Behaved like the young, impressionable girl she was?

Courtney bit her lip until it hurt. There was no need denying it any longer. At first she had tried to impress him because he was so interesting. But now she knew she was head-over-heels in love with him. God had providence over everything that was good, Clint said. And this was good! But something was holding them apart.

Raising her eyes to his, she saw the melancholy there that had formed a tight ring around her heart. And then she stopped breathing. The other woman . . . it had to be . . .

"Alexis Worthington—who is she, Clint?" Courtney's voice was so low and filled with hurt that she wondered how Clint heard. But he did, because he groaned. Then, letting go of her hand, he turned away, wiping uselessly at the rebellious kink of sun-bronzed hair beneath the band of his wide-brimmed hat. Even from a side view, his jawline showed its formidable strength. What could threaten that?

When Clint spoke, his voice was as impersonal as if he were discussing the weather. "Alexis Worthington is now Alexis Villard—"

"But she told me—" Courtney blurted out without thinking.

"You saw her! What did she say or do to you?"

Seeing that Clint's face was drained of color, Courtney told of the brief encounter on the stairway as if there were nothing out of the ordinary. It seemed inappropriate to make mention of their hot exchange of words.

Clint's question came as a surprise. "What was she doing there?"

"Why—why, she—Miss Worthington—Mrs. Villard

was going upstairs to pick up something she had left—"

"Stop stalling, Courtney," Clint said gently. "Alexis could have left nothing because she had not been in the house."

Wide-eyed, Courtney looked at him. "Are you sure? She said she left her gloves in your room."

"She did," he said grimly, "on that trip—to plant the gloves for whatever reason. I saw her at the mine briefly, that's all. Her father was the former co-owner of one of the Kennedy silver mines, and she inherited a small share. Then," Clint paused, and Courtney was sure he was unaware of the bitterness in his voice, "that was not enough—so she eloped with Cyril Villard of the Villard Railroad Company."

Courtney did not doubt Clint's words. But neither was she comforted. Alexis had said they were sweethearts. Oh, how had this subject come up? Like a serpent in a Garden of Purity, it had reared its ugly head. The beautiful moment was gone . . .

She made no protest when Clint lifted her lightly onto the little mare. A certain nameless fear filled her heart.

CHAPTER 17

Unexpected Faces

Without warning, the sky darkened. Dust of a peculiar color put the sun in near-total eclipse. The trees were behind them now, and ahead, against a bare mountain, was a gaping hole. Bewhiskered men filled in the spaces where an endless stretch of stumps said that trees had been cut.

Courtney knew even before the welcoming calls of "Hi'ya, Bossman!" that this must be Cousin Bella's mine. Or, at least, a part of what (she was to learn later) comprised the Kennedy Company, for beyond where the layer of dust was thinner, she had spotted dozens of the caves.

It was all very new and very frightening. The men (and even the mules, it seemed) were staring at her. Even with Clint's massive shoulders between her and the spectators, she felt the screws of apprehension turn more tightly around her heart. There was the distinct feeling of being watched by one or several pairs of eyes, more with purpose than curiosity.

There was no escape. Several men had surrounded Clint and were asking questions she did not understand. Trying to calm herself, Courtney turned her eyes to a clearing ahead. If she could force her gaze high enough, maybe there would be a hole in the choking dust. There was. But it revealed no patch of sapphire sky—just tall, tall mountains of granite, unbroken by greenery.

Slowly she lowered her eyes, meeting the eyes of a stranger—a stranger who was stalking her . . . there could be no doubt. But who? Why? He was dusty all over. His face, beneath a dust-whitened, week-old stubble on his cheeks and chin, was cross-grained from exposure to the sun. His hat was pulled low and, to her horror, she saw that he was fingering a rifle strapped to his saddle.

And then he grinned, the kind of grin that was an insult to a young lady. Suddenly it was as if the dust closed in around her, filling her lungs, stealing her breath. The man's face—something she herself was unable to identify—was vaguely familiar. The grin turned to a leer before she could gather the strength to touch Clint's sleeve.

"Clint!" She whispered. "Clint—"

Courtney raised a shaking finger to point. But the man was gone. "I—I feel a little faint—"

"How thoughtless of me!" Clint said in apology. He turned toward the clearing immediately, telling her about the machinery. But she heard none of it. Her mind was on the strange figure and his threat to her, for she was certain that this was not a chance encounter.

Courtney was unaware that they had stopped until Clint said, "We'll go in here for a minute, if you don't mind. Aunt Bella told Ahab about her favorite cousin, and he's eager to meet you."

Ahab turned out to be the company smithy. Her first glimpse made Courtney want to smile. He was short but powerfully built, with big muscles rippling up and down the hairy arms. His head was round and flat, resembling a pumpkin, and his eyes—squinting from whorls of wrinkles—looked as if they had been stuck in as an afterthought, two tiny blue beads. But they sparkled with ready laughter, and his voice, even though he spoke with a clipped accent, was as thick and sweet as Mandy's hive-fresh honey.

"Well, now, Missy, ain't it a privilege though?"

Awkwardly Ahab tried to wipe the soot from his blackened hands, using a ragged bandanna that he had suspended from the bib of his worn leather apron. Examining his hands and finding them no cleaner, the smithy ran his stubby fingers through sweat-matted hair in despair.

Smiling, Courtney extended her hand. "It is good to make your acquaintance, Mr. Ahab, Sir."

"Well, now, Clint, ain't she a real lady? Shakin' hands with the likes o' me!"

And to emphasize his point, Ahab slapped his other hand on top of Courtney's. Then immediately he led the way to the fiery forge and his anvils, where (he said with pride) two young men were assigned to him as apprentices. Not likely a sweet young thing like her would be needin' to have a horse shod . . . still and all, it depended on what her plans were?

Clint spoke for her. "We aren't going to let go of her—ever. See you in church tomorrow, Ahab?"

"If the creek'll take off this soot 'twixt now and meetin' time!" The merry eyes danced as Clint and

Courtney turned to go. "Good y're here, Missy—very, very good!"

As soon as they were out of sight, Clint pulled an enormous bandanna from his pocket. Rub as he would, the smudges remained on Courtney's hands, just as Clint's words remained in her heart. "What a little trouper you are, Courtney Glamora," he said softly. "They expected you to be a snob and you're winning the hearts of the Columbia Territory!"

Courtney began to enjoy herself. She was listening raptly now and learning that the Kennedy Company included a company store and a church, in addition to the blacksmith shop. Workers, Clint explained, purchased small shares if they chose, and all merchandise came to them at cost. How exciting!

And the company store was indeed an eyeful for a young lady who was only vaguely aware that there was a word called *shopping*. It was something servants did—or so she had thought.

The split-log building had a rough floor of unplaned boards. Courtney looked around her in dismay at the coils of wire and rope hanging from the rafters, with sticky flypaper—in long curled streamers—hung haphazardly between. The walls were strung with buckets, hoes, rakes, all kinds of dried beans in sacks, and long strips of what looked like the dried venison Clint had called jerky. Counters crisscrossed each other throughout the store, their countless shelves stacked with strange hardware—something to be used in the mines, Courtney supposed. A small wood stove was near the back of the barnlike building, and around it barrels galore.

"Set on one o' them barrels iffen you like," a passing customer said. "Makin' sure y' put th' lid on first. Had one woman near drown in the pickle barrel once—some fine lady from th' city. 'Nother time ole Jed Tomlinson had hisself a snort o' fire-water and plum fell into th' flour barrel. Word 'ad it 'twas powerful hard gettin' 'im out—him bein' so fat 'n all. Customers found 'is stickpin and chewin' tobacco in th' flour fer months. Folks had t' sift it! Well, I best be buyin' my ole lady some calico—hope I did'n offend y' none."

Courtney shook her head without ever meeting the man's eyes. She was fascinated with the scene in back. The stove, squatted on its haunches, looked like a rabbit trying to escape through the maze of oil barrels, molasses kegs, an open cracker barrel, and the mile-high stacks of fruits and vegetables beneath a crudely lettered sign saying LOCAL PRODUCE. Somebody must have helped the proprietor with the spelling. She repressed a smile at the spelling on the labels of the produce.

Tony Bronson bowed kindly when Clint presented him to Courtney, but he did not let go of an armful of sacked coffee beans he was uncrating. He was a big man with a kind face and an eye for business. Looking Courtney up and down, he obviously decided against steering her toward the dry goods.

"My wife's dyin' to meetcha, Miz Courtney. She'll be seein' you at church, come tomorrow." Tony shelved the coffee bags, exhaled in relief, and then added with an attempt at humor. "That is, providin' her new dress's done!"

Other customers drifted in, and Courtney picked her way cautiously through the clutter. Tony, still panting, had asked if the two men could talk alone "a spell." And not sure how long that was, she would examine the "Bargin Korner" out of curiosity.

Some of the items were much higher than her head, and in a matter of moments she was out of sight.

That accounted for her overhearing a part of a conversation intended for neither her ears nor Clint's. It was wrong to eavesdrop, and Courtney tried to pull herself away. But at the mention of Alexis Worthington Villard's name, she made herself even smaller—half-wishing she were not here, yet having no power to announce her presence.

"Yeah, she's back, 'n I'd be guessin' t' stay, perish th' thought! That woman's trouble fer th' Kennedys. Allus made me madder'n a hornet when folks said them two was right fer one another—"

The man's voice dropped, and Courtney strained to hear what the person to whom he spoke would say. She did not have to wait long. "Well, you wuz right! Never was much between 'em anyway—leastwise not on her part. Any woman who'd leave a man like that—and fer th' Villard money—"

"Ain't y' heard? Villard and Company's gone bust like Holladay! So that connivin' woman's dumped th' man she thought wuz monied. Like as not, she's back fer more'n t' check on her part. She could make it bigger, y' know, by gettin' 'er claws on Clint agin—"

"May th' Almighty forbid!"

The men were moving away, and it was hard for Courtney to hear anything except fragments. "Th' woman's a real witch . . . what she done t' that pore unfortunate boy . . . startin' them tales 'bout him bein' possessed by a devil . . . no, name ain't Kennedy . . . right noble o' them takin' 'im in . . . well, she ain't gittin' Clint . . . Miss Bella's tooken care o'that . . ."

Courtney hardly knew when Clint came for her.

As if from a long way off, she heard him say he had planned that the two of them would tour The-Church-in-the-Wildwood, but there was too little time. "You know Aunt Bella's rules!"

Forcing a smile, Courtney went out with him to where the two mares waited. Her legs felt weak and she was a bit faint. But what she saw could be no illusion. Nobody had red hair that flamed like that except Alexis. And she—she was talking to the man who had been watching Courtney. Clint did not see.

CHAPTER 18

Welcome Home!

It took several hours for Courtney to put aside puzzling questions and drop into a troubled sleep. In it the questions became nocturnal creatures—giant owls that filled the branches of the Douglas fir trees outside her window, beating their wide, feathered wings against the panes, twisting their neckless heads round and round. . . hissing. . . screeching. . . hooting in mockery. . . the pale eyes focused on her. . . the talons open and ready to grab her, choke her.

Who. . . Who. . . WHO? the evil phantoms hooted. *Who is the stranger? What does he want of you? What does the woman want of you? Who. . . who. . . WHO are you? And why are you here? Why did one send you away. . . another send for you. . . and who. . . who. . . WHO is the innocent-eyed man calling himself a Kennedy? Why are you here? Who is enemy and who is friend? Who. . . who. . . WHO. . . ?*

She awoke soaked with cold sweat. For the first time she was lonely and afraid. As frightened as she was, however, there must be no sleep. Asleep, one had no command of the brain. These questioning creatures could claim her as their own—and the mysteries would never be solved. But did it matter so much? She was tired. . . so tired. . . and, fight as she would, Courtney surrendered, letting slumber enfold her in darkness.

Dawn was still only a pale rose promise when the clatter of pots and pans downstairs and the rattle of carriage wheels outside the window awakened Courtney. Weary as she was, it was a relief to hear human voices. Quickly she drew the heavy drapes aside, and in the dim light she could make out the figures of two men. Thankfully, she saw that they were Clint and Donolar. And then she saw that the box on back of the vehicle was piled high with roses.

Full consciousness came slowly. Yes, of course, this was Sunday. It made sense that the boy—*man*—would furnish flowers for the service. And, she remembered as she felt for her slippers, the best time for picking them was when the petals were still damp with dew.

Cousin Bella, regal in a black suit and hat with a white ostrich plume, went about the seating in the carriage as methodically as she had at the dining room. Nobody ever crossed her, Courtney supposed, focusing her eyes on the metal chain suspended around her cousin's neck, holding a silver cross that must have weighed a pound. Glancing at Clint, she saw that he was smiling in endorsement when his aunt said the two of them should sit in front.

"Without a chaperone?"

Clint whispered the teasing words, but Cousin Bella overheard. "I was never one for convention," she said, lifting her skirt and stepping into the carriage unaided. "Imagine dictating to ladies how many petticoats to wear! Of course, some of the rules for men were made by addleheads, too. Take the one about its being against the law for *men* to spit tobacco juice, which," she sniffed, "must make it perfectly acceptable a practice for the fairer sex!"

There was laughter. Donolar climbed into the back seat with Cousin Bella. Mandy and Mrs. Rueben would be along in the buggy as soon as Sunday dinner was done.

Conscious of the riders behind, Courtney held herself in a stiffly correct posture. Carefully, she kept her face averted. But she was glad that she had taken care with her grooming and knew that her efforts had not been in vain.

When the two behind them engaged in conversation, Clint spoke. "You look different—older," he said.

Good! He had noticed. Courtney had chosen a pink-striped dress and her black basque. But she was reasonably sure that it was neither the clothing nor the tiny high-topped boots with the fringe around the top that caused Clint to see her as more grown-up. It was her hair. It was the first time he had seen her shining, black tresses in a braided coronet.

There was no more talk between them. "My, my! What a crowd! Better wheel the carriage under these trees, Clint," Cousin Bella was saying.

"They all want to see Miss Courtney," Donolar said in a small, shy voice.

Courtney turned to face him and saw adoration in the wide, innocent eyes. "You may call me Courtney," she said.

There was delight in his smile. "Wait until I tell the butterflies!" he exclaimed, then added meekly,

"I promised them you would come for a visit. They will accept you. The roses do."

Poor Donolar. He touched her heart, and certainly she must visit his garden. He was such a riddle in her mind.

"Lift your skirts a bit, Courtney. We'll have to pick our way through these wagons like rabbits in a briarpatch. Brother Jim's going to have himself a houseful." Cousin Bella's tone was one of satisfaction.

The weathered church, with a spire that pierced the sky, was larger inside than one would guess. It looked small tucked away in the grove of enormous trees. And it had seen a lot of use, judging by the scars of hobnail boots on the worn boards of the floor.

Cousin Bella was right about the size of the congregation. The women—all older than Courtney—looked very much the same, as if their cotton dresses and matching poke bonnets were cut from the same pattern and often-identical design. Or had life here simply weathered them as it had the church? But they sat straight, unbent by hardship or storm.

There was more variation among the men. Some wore proper dark suits with stiff, high-necked collars. But the others! Why, there were some occupying the scarred benches who had never heard the word *bath* and obviously saw no reason for changing clothes *ever*. Did they really know that buckskins *smelled*, and that only filthy, unshaven men wore them to church? Those must be trappers with the coonskin caps and knee-high moccasins, their jaws puffed out like tobacco pouches. Courtney recognized the prospectors from those she had seen on the train. Still full-bearded, the men had dressed up for the Sunday service by tying their shoulder-length hair back with colored strings and splashing water at the locks above the eyebrows, giving the look that they had fallen into a rain barrel. But it was the miners who captured her attention. Several of them she recognized. It was unbecoming to stare—maybe even dangerous. Courtney had tried to put Clint's warning aside, but it surfaced at a time like this. Could he—that man who stared at her so leeringly and then engaged Alexis in conversation—be here?

Someone sounded a pitch pipe, and the congregation burst into song with more vigor than talent. As she had done on the train, Courtney listened, and soon was singing with them the words to "Beulah Land."

Clint took her hand when the invocation began. Courtney felt her fingers tremble and was thankful that all heads were bowed. She would not wish any of them to read what was in her eyes.

An enormous man who looked far too big for his suit walked with a heavy tread to the hand-hewn pulpit. The atmosphere was one of expectancy. The others knew what to expect, but Courtney did not, and later she suspected that had Mrs. Thorpe been here, the governess would have told her to close her mouth!

The gorilla of a man (hadn't Cousin Bella called him "Brother Jim"?) stripped off his tie, then the removable collar of his shirt. Striding back and forth on the stage, he shoved both hands into the pockets of his suit pants. And then he began flailing away at the air like some windup toy whose spring had suddenly popped.

"Brothers and sisters, is it well with thee? Is it well

with the man who gambles away his wage whilst his wife and children go begging? Is it well with the man who gulps down the rotgut made by some of the moonshiners, taking the risk of being a rocking, reeling, vomiting drunk teetering around on the rim of hell? No, I tell you, ten thousand times no!"

"*No. . . no. . . NO!*" The words came from every corner.

"Now, good brethren, going to church don't make a man a Christian soldier any more than going into a stable makes a man a horse!"

"*Amen. . . amen. . . AMEN!*"

Courtney's insides were knotted into a little wad, and her bones, she was sure, had dissolved. Surely this was a continuation of last night's terrifying dreams.

Clint must have seen her pale face. He reached for her hand and held it securely between his until she could feel the blood begin to course through her fingers.

"I should have prepared you, darling," Clint whispered against her ear so softly she could scarcely hear. "Brother Jim's a retired prize-fighter who believes in slugging it out bare-fisted with the devil."

Courtney relaxed enough to turn an appreciative half-smile at Clint. But she was sure he read the trouble in her eyes. It was not Brother Jim alone who disturbed her. He was frightening but somewhat amusing, and totally lovable in his battle against sin. It was something else. It was life—the good and bad of it. And the battle she was fighting within herself—alone. The dream had brought the loneliness back.

Courtney realized suddenly that the preacher's tone had changed completely. "Is it well with thee?" Softly this time. "Of course not. You can't go toting that heavy knapsack of burdens alone. Get right with God. He'll lift every care from that sack, drown them in the Columbia, and fill it with something called *love*...love for Him...for thy neighbor ...and thyself. Peace...Peace...peace He leaves with us..."

Last night's dreams dissipated. Courtney felt a soft-sweet peace fill her heart—almost overpowering, like the scent of Donolar's roses. The smile she turned on Clint was radiant.

The service was over. People crowded around Courtney in a way that made her sure Cousin Bella had prepared them. "Welcome home!" they were saying. And whether these kind people meant the mansion or the church was of no consequence. She was *home*!

CHAPTER 19
In the Garden

The peace lingered in Courtney's heart, a peace that seemed to have no point of beginning. Was it on the train when Clint explained the providence of God? When he took her hand that first night and prayed for her? Peace did not start with the antics of Brother Jim, who strung adjectives the way a necklace-maker strings beads and created verbal gems that shook the "evildoers" he addressed. Nor did it start with his challenges to "get in the ring" with the infidel (rolling up his sleeves), either. But, yes, his soft-spoken ending about God's love and the peace it would bring may have let bloom the seed her father had planted so long ago and that Clint, Cousin Bella, and this country had nourished.

The somber atmosphere she had sensed on arrival no longer prevailed. There was quietness in the Mansion, but it held no brooding menace—the herald of disaster that Courtney had felt at Waverly Manor. The difference was love. But she must write home, though it was duty without love. . .

Cousin Bella had encouraged Courtney to familiarize herself with the library, as they would be working with some of the material. This in answer to Courtney's concerned question as to when her duties as a companion would begin. There was a wealth of information which she could use for reference in her letters to Efraim and Lance. Sadly, she realized that she did not have much to write to Mother. Courtney knew only that she had spoken of Vanessa's need for her. "I must be growing up, Lord," she whispered at the thought, "it doesn't hurt so much anymore."

Courtney had found no time for reading or writing. She and Clint had ridden over every acre of the Kennedy estate, since Cousin Bella had wanted her to see the land and meet the people. It must all be very important to her cousin, as she had asked Clint to be here instead of at the mines. Well, Clint would be leaving tomorrow (but he would be back for the weekends, he told her, when Courtney surprised herself by objecting). He had his work, and she had hers. She would get down to the business for which Arabella Kennedy had sent for her.

She wandered into the library, examined a few books, and started to open the family Bible when it occurred to her that there would hardly be time to dig as deeply as she wished. It was a brilliant June day. Clint had told her not to ride about the countryside alone, but surely a short walk was all right.

Without realizing that she had a destination in mind, Courtney turned toward Donolar's garden. He was busy, picking off rose hips from the roses whose petals had fallen. He saw her from a distance. "Why, Courtney!" he called while she was yet a long way off. "The roses will be so happy. I told them you would come."

They walked among the flowers. Surely there must be one of every variety in the world, and Donolar knew the names of them all. The butterflies brought seeds from across the ocean, he said—some of them from the King's Castle.

The garden was larger than Courtney had realized. Carefully pruned back as they were, some of the bushes reached above her head. "Don't be afraid, Courtney," Donolar said soothingly. "I am taller. I can see over."

It had not occurred to Courtney to be afraid, but his words caused her heart to beat a little faster. But her apprehension lessened as the boy talked. The scent of the sun beating down on the pines mingled with the heady perfume of the roses. And just a stone's throw away, the little brook was singing a hymn. Why, she was safer than safe here. This was Innisfree!

So she gave him her undivided attention when he related to her what the butterflies told her about the roses. Roses were "love blossoms." A cabbage rose sent to a lady meant the young man was "beholding." And red roses? Oh, the deeper the color, the deeper the love . . .

He stopped suddenly. "Someday I will tell you all the names—and their secrets. Shakespeare was wrong—names make roses smell sweeter. Like my name—being a Kennedy makes me better than I am—"

"No, Donolar," Courtney said, turning to retrace her steps, "I agree with Shakespeare. You would have been just as dear by any other name."

The boy's face all but obscured the sun with its

brightness. "You are so nice, Courtney—and I will tell you all I know. Names *do* matter—I am glad Mrs. Villard's name is not Alexis Desmond. And it is good that your name is Glamora instead of Bellevue—"

Courtney stopped with such suddenness that Donolar, his arms laden with roses, stopped just short of bumping into her. Whirling to face him, "Bellevue!" she whispered. "How did you know the name?"

The childish face twitched with emotion, and for a moment Courtney felt that he was about to reveal a secret. Then the innocent face went blank and the great, oval eyes lost the faint flicker of expression. He was Donolar again.

"The woods are full of secrets. The butterflies sometimes leave my garden and they tell me. You should not walk alone—"

"Courtney's earlier apprehension returned. Turning away, she walked with quickened step, feeling somewhat relieved when she reached the rose-wound arch of the garden gate.

"I will see you this evening," Courtney said with a departing wave.

"And Doc George will dine with us—he floats in like my butterflies." Donolar's announcement came as naturally as if the conversation had centered around the man for whom Cousin Bella reserved a chair at her table.

CHAPTER 20
End of Togetherness

Dinner was a pleasure, the only flaw for Courtney being that tomorrow ended a beautiful period of togetherness for her and Clint. With him, she had grown so much, changed so much. Not that she had to prove it, Clint had teased, by sweeping her hair up into the coronet—and, promptly, upon their arrival home from church that day, pulling the pins from the braids and allowing her dark hair to cascade down her shoulders.

Tonight it obviously pleased him that Courtney wore it in the girlishly demure style. Aware that his eyes were on her, she turned away to study the profile of their guest. She had had only a vague impression of a rotund, Santa-faced man as introductions were made and diners seated. Now she saw that Dr. George Washington Lovelace (affectionately addressed as "Doc George" by his friends—elsewhere as well as here, Courtney suspected) was more interesting and more complex than the first glance indicated.

He smelled of pills that even the roses could not overpower. His hair, although turned white by time, was as full as a cloud, giving his bare head the look of an oversized snowball. The neatly trimmed beard, just as white, swept upward to meet muttonchops which extended to the hairline. But beneath the whiteness were round, rosy cheeks, and above it a pair of merry blue eyes. A Santa who dispensed pills. Courtney smiled at the thought.

To her embarrassment, the doctor saw. "Ah, my dear, something amuses you? It is good to see a smile on that rather sad face. As your cousin said, you are a lovely young lady—a trifle on the lean side. Are you well?"

"Quite well, thank you, Sir." Courtney concentrated on unfolding her napkin as Mandy set the venison roast before Doc George, the apparent host.

Thinking that this ended the subject, Courtney turned a shy smile to Clint. But the subject was not closed.

"You will be one of us, I understand, and I take care of the needs of the body in this household." Courtney wondered how he knew if she would be staying when she did not know herself. He hardly looked like a man who sipped with the bees or communed with the butterflies, but it was Donolar—not Cousin Bella—who had known he would join them. With a flourish he unfolded the enormous white napkin beside his plate and tucked one corner above the top button of his vest. He took the carving knife in one dimpled hand and the fork in the other, using them for gesturing as he spoke.

"Prepare for surgery!" he announced, and proceeded with his self-introduction before carving.

Dr. George Washington Lovelace, he said of

himself, had no "real class," but plenty of history. He was a part of history, having grown up here on the frontier with his good friend Arabella Kennedy. After all, this land was named for the nation's first President, and, although there were dozens of namesakes since the Columbia Territory became a state, none of these in Washington save himself boasted a degree in medicine. However, folks did not take kindly to "newfangled drugs," so the sign at his office door read HOMEOPATHIC MEDICINE.

"Yep!" he said when at length he began carving generous slices from the brown roast, "Here in our settlement we look after one another. The Kennedys keep folks' bellies full. I look after the flesh—and my sidekick, Big Jimbo, is responsible for the souls! The devil's got no real friends hereabouts."

"You weren't at church Sunday, George Washington," Cousin Bella reminded him.

"Right you are," he answered, laying down the carving set. "Satan detained me. Ran into—well, some trouble. Sure needed that hard-punching preacher with me. His hellfire sermons scare the weasel-eyed crooks more than any officer of the law. They come riding in here with a toothpick, but Big Jimbo there goes after them with a crowbar of words! Good man—if he had his way every saloon in this state would be so dry the drunks would have to be primed to spit!"

There was laughter. "Right you are, George Washington," Cousin Bella agreed. "Brother Jim's not one to speak of the Bible in terms of a halfway house. It's God or nothing! And, now, shall we eat?"

In contrast to Doc George's near-tirade of hot words, his prayer was soft and gentle. One phrase in particular appealed to Courtney: "Let us love one another as You have loved us . . ."

The evening was serving to make Courtney feel more and more a part of the new country. She had known very little about what went on in the Eastern town in which she lived, and not much more about her own home. Yet here she was in the midst of a moral and spiritual crusade she had never known existed.

There was small talk. Then suddenly Donolar interrupted quietly. "Doc George, your trouble—the one Satan sent—was it The Brothers?"

The doctor's rose cheeks paled slightly. "Yes, Boy, it was. But, for now, tell me—what kind of roses are these?"

Something had gone amiss. Courtney felt it. And yet she was unable to put the puzzle together. She would have to think about it later as the group was in the midst of goodbyes.

"Did they wear you out?" Clint asked with concern as he pulled her chair from the table. Not at all, she told him, thrilling to the touch of his hands holding hers for so long.

But her ears had picked up snatches of another conversation. That "redhead" was up to no good, Doc said. And Cousin Bella added, "Cunning as a fox . . . shrewd . . . coldly calculating. Love? Pshaw, she doesn't know the definition . . . but if my plan works . . . and it will!"

CHAPTER 21

Just As I Am!

Courtney lay staring at the ceiling in the darkness. Sleep seemed light-years away with so many things on her mind. There was something unsatisfactory about Clint's goodbye, although she hardly knew what she had expected. He had seemed a bit preoccupied at dinner—understandable with Doc George talking nonstop. But in their last moments together, his lightness seemed forced, and she had the feeling that something was worrying him. When she asked him, Clint shrugged it off.

"Nothing—only I wish we could have talked."

Courtney had laughed, which threw the conversation awry. Clint visibly relaxed, told her to reserve that laugh just for him since he loved the sound of Christmas bells, and then—with such a tight squeeze of her hands that it was painful—turned and walked away. Courtney started to follow and then decided against it. Now, alone in her darkened bedroom, she wished with all her heart that she had. *Oh, Clint*, her heart cried out.

Well, she consoled herself, they would be together on weekends...

With that thought, another surfaced—memory of the talk between Cousin Bella and Doc George. It was clear enough who the "redhead" was. It had to be Alexis. And it was just as clear that neither of them trusted her presence here. Was it because of her holdings in the mine? Surely they did not entertain the idea that Clint was interested in her. And, anyway, wasn't she married?

Courtney fluffed her pillow and found a more comfortable position. But still the thoughts came. What, she wondered, did this worldly-wise woman think of divorce? If Alexis took the "forsaking all others" vow and broke it, that was dangerous in more ways than one, wasn't it? She would be breaking a covenant. And she would risk the fury of Brother Jim, who would call her a harlot...but what if she *didn't* divorce this Villard? Courtney was no match for her.

How silly! Alexis Worthington Villard was not going to get her claws in Clint. He was not interested. He had made that clear. And, well, Courtney thought with a wicked little grin, there were times when even a Madonna-like young lady took matters into her own hands. Hadn't she proved that on the train?

The train! She had been on the rim of slumber when memory of the robbery came. Without preamble, it all flashed before her eyes. Behind closed lids, Courtney saw the man whom Clint had threatened to expose, saw recognition in Clint's eyes and knew without question that it was the same robber's face she had seen at the mine and again as he spoke with Alexis.

Other pieces fell around her like confetti then. There were no missing parts. There could be no doubt as to the man's identity. Clint had spoken of his half-brothers, the Bellevues. Then there was Donolar's question, "Was it The Brothers?" and the way Doc George turned the matter aside. It was something they all knew, but something they did not discuss, particularly when it would cast shame on the family tied in with both Clint and Courtney. Courtney could get no farther in her thinking. It probably had something to do with the mines, with money, with jealousy—all those evil things. This was nothing she could settle. But she knew who could!

"Hello, Lord, Your Honor! Now, be patient with me while I learn to address You properly—and while I get to know Your Son. I was a pilgrim here at the Mansion-in-the-Wild and again at the Church in the Wildwood...and I am a pilgrim Up There with You. I have learned how to love, Lord. Now You teach me to trust—have faith in how You settle things down here. Make all the things grow inside my heart that should be there. And, in the meanwhile, I will serve You just as I am..."

Feeling content just as she was for the first time in her life, Courtney Glamora slept.

CHAPTER 22
Letters Home

Time was passing, Courtney realized. Even Cousin Bella was aware.

"It will be lonely without Clint." Cousin Bella was spooning honey on a biscuit as the two of them had breakfast in the little nook overlooking Donolar's garden.

It was hard to tell whether the words were a statement or a question. Biting into the biscuit, her cousin continued, "We must make the most of the time that he is away. Do you feel up to some work?"

Courtney did.

It was not very difficult—very pleasant, really. There was a need to go with the family history. And there were letters to write.

"Would you mind very much if, before my duties commence, I write to my family?" Courtney asked.

Cousin Bella looked a bit agitated. Courtney had the feeling that the extraordinarily careful blotting of her lips with the fringed napkin was a delaying tactic. Oh, she did hope that she had not offended

Cousin Bella. After all, her cousin had a purpose in sending for her. She must be prepared to fulfill it. It was her duty to give up the freedom she had known, the carefree days of riding, talking, and laughing with Clint . . . visiting in the "other world" of Donolar's roses . . . wandering through the mysterious rooms of the Mansion . . . and just plain daydreaming about a pair of blue-lake eyes . . .

When at length Cousin Bella spoke, her words surprised Courtney. "Your family? Yes, you must write Efraim, of course. But have you not been happy here?"

Courtney found the question strange. "Oh, yes, Cousin Bella! It has been the happiest time of my life—"

The fading dark eyes of the older woman bored into the velvet depths of the younger. "I was hoping," she said slowly, "that you had come to think of *us* as your family. Am I asking too much, Courtney? It is with good reason that I ask!"

At the moment the reason did not trouble Courtney. She was too astounded at her reaction to Cousin Bella's words. Why, yes, of *course* this was home. Home—a *real* home—had God for an architect. He built it on love and security—something she had never had as a child. And here it was in the middle of the wilderness. "Doesn't God work in mysterious ways?" She said aloud. At her words, Cousin Bella dabbed at her eyes with a lace handkerchief. And Courtney knew that she was happy to be here no matter what the reason.

• • •

Courtney deliberated long before beginning her

letters to the two men in her life—before Clint. It hardly seemed fair to tell them that she had found happiness here. Why not spend her words on subjects that would interest them most? Efraim surely would wish to know something of their family history, and she was already fairly well-informed about it. Lance, whom she thought of as "family," would be inspired by the unspoiled beauty of the land. In neither case did Courtney plan to make mention of either Clint or Donolar. Asked why, she would have been able to give no answer.

Family. Courtney picked up her pen and then laid it back down on the cherrywood writing desk. She wondered if her brother would understand the change in her, the gradual maturation into young womanhood, her new emotional ties, and her acquaintance with God as a "Person." Cousin Bella had made it clear that "bloodline relatives" were but a small part of one's *real* family. "They're sort of pushed off on us, you know, while friends are those who love you no matter what you are or aren't. The church is the family that counts!"

In a way she was right, Courtney supposed. Cousin Bella was very wise. Take those Bellevue Brothers—Courtney shuddered and decided against making mention of them, too.

> *My very dear Efraim,* she wrote, *first I must inquire about your health. But, then, I know you are well, because you come from such sturdy stock . . .*

He would be interested, Courtney told him, to learn of their distant—oh, *very* distant—kin to the reverend Dr. John McLoughlin. She described the painting which hung in the library, entitled "White Eagle." Small wonder the Indians so named their ancestor with snow-white hair flowing to his shoulders and piercing eyes beneath bushy brows! She supposed he would be called a furrier, but the Indians around the mouth of the river were useless as hunters. He built a fort in what was now Vancouver, Washington. Some had no idea, Cousin Bella had said, that the fort included a schoolhouse and chapel as well as a powder magazine of brick and stone. And in the center was the Governor's mansion—two stories high. The clerks, chaplain, physician, and "help" dined together on substantial, several-course dinners. . .

> *And, Efraim, our cousin continues the practice to this day. We all eat together: the cook, the housekeeper, and the wayfaring stranger. Such a nice, cozy feeling. She commands, but regally. . . .*

Come to think of it, Cousin Bella just may have borrowed some of her ways from Cousin John's (many times removed) widow, the grand "First Lady" who behaved more like a queen. Lady McLoughlin wore brilliant colors, according to the books, but Cousin Bella might very well be a black-and-white version.

The house was rather a nightmare, part of it being remains of the brick foundation of the McLoughlin house, some of which had been destroyed by flood and some by fire. But the foundation stood as an east wing of the house. The west wing was built later by Cousin Bella's grandfather, then badly damaged by an Indian raid, but now repaired. The rest of the rambling maze was the actual handwork of Cousin Arabella Kennedy's father and remained the object of her pride. Outside, the Mansion-in-the-Wild looked dilapidated—more like pictures of farmhouses they had seen, with only a pepper-pot tower to give it the claim to royalty.

But the inside—oh, Efraim, how wonderfully old and preserved. "I doubt if I have seen all the rooms . . . polished wood . . . fireplaces . . . imported tapestry . . . absolutely the personification of antiquity . . . which adds a feel of mystery . . ."

Courtney was exhausted. Laying down the pen, she flexed her fingers and decided to leave the mines for another time. Coal mines had caused their family so much grief, and she must be careful to say nothing that would make the same sound true of the silver mines—nothing that would keep him away.

But there was one more subject. It could not be avoided.

> *Next week I will be 17, Efraim. If I were home, I suppose Mother would be making arrangements for my debut as she did for Vanessa.* Courtney paused, wondering how to go on. *Oh, Efraim, where IS our mother? Is something wrong? . . . I am frightened . . .*

She sealed the letter, then picked up another sheet of Cousin Bella's pale blue paper. The note she wrote to Lance was brief—mostly about a mountain stream that dropped over 600 feet, in two graceful leaps, from the Columbia River gorge to the river level below. How lovely it would be captured on canvas.

He would have to see this land to believe its beauty. Should she sign it "With Love?" Courtney hesitated, and then closed the short note with "Sincerely." Neither sounded right.

CHAPTER 23
The Birthday Gift

After mailing Efraim's letter, Courtney wondered if she had embellished a bit. No, not really. The pieced-together Mansion was splendid in a crumbling sort of way. The walls had grown friendly with her, and—like Donolar's roses—endeavored, it seemed, to whisper their ancient secrets. My goodness, she *had* fallen under its spell!

Cousin Bella, like the walls, appeared often on the verge of divulging some secret. Then, as they worked together in the library, Courtney would decide she had only imagined that part of it. A lifted eyebrow would cause the purposeful woman to dig into the books with something that resembled fury.

They talked on occasion—always warm, always friendly, but somehow leaving something unsaid. Courtney had a feeling that it had something to do with the third reason among those that Cousin Bella had mentioned for wanting her to come here . . . or were those reasons contrived? It hurt to remember that her cousin had let it slip that Mother had asked the distant relative to take her daughter off her hands.

"Did you tell Efraim about your new friends here?" Cousin Bella asked once as they finished one day's work.

"Not a great deal," Courtney said, neatly stacking the papers and hoping they would not pursue the subject. It was all so complex. How could she explain the people she had come to love here? They were all so wonderful. But put on paper, they might sound like objects of ridicule—the way Mother had made "those primitive people Out West" sound.

Courtney was concerned needlessly. When Cousin Bella spoke, it was about a different matter. "I—I find this a trifle awkward," she began, then paused. It was the first time Courtney had heard her hesitate to speak her mind. "But—well—do you know who is handling the Glamora fortune?"

Courtney frowned. She had never given much thought to money. It was simply a medium of exchange. For goods. For favors. And, yes, in her mother's circle, for *love*! There *was* a lawyer, she remembered. A Mr. Levitt? But Efraim was studying law and—

She broke off in midsentence. Cousin Bella did not appear to be listening. Would this be a good time to ask more of her mother? But, no, Efraim would tell her.

Cousin Bella demanded far less of her time than Courtney had expected. There was time to read and memorize a few of the underlined passages in the family Bible. Time, too, to study the detailed family tree, some of it written laboriously in fading pencil, some in spidery manuscript, and some in block printing—but all very detailed. The paper was crisp with age, and Courtney had to be very careful lest it fall apart as she ran a finger through the lists of births, marriages, and deaths. At length she found what she wanted—the union of Ana Bellevue and Gabriel Glamora.

She didn't know why, but it seemed important that she find her own name. It was a special identity, such as Clint's calling her Courtney in his prayer.

Here! Here were the births. But her finger went no farther than Efraim, the firstborn. The dates were right but the spacing was not. Just below Efraim's statistics another name had been entered at one time—entered and then half-erased. Try as she would, there was no making out the blurred words. If there had been another child, Efraim would know, and there would be no reason to keep it secret.

A sudden step on the stair caused Courtney to jump and close the Bible guiltily. If the words were intended for her eyes, they would not have been erased. She wished she were able to erase her niggling questions and doubts as easily.

"Courtney!" It was Cousin Bella's voice. "Why do you close yourself in on so lovely a day, child? I was going to surprise you—but seeing that you are here—"

She pulled a large bouquet of wildflowers from behind her back. Handing them to Courtney, she said, "Aren't they lovely?" but her voice sounded a little false.

Clint had sent them by the son of one of the miners, she said, and then retreated hurriedly.

A note was tucked between the tall spikes of purple lupine and fern: "I am so sorry, dear Courtney, that it is impossible for me to be with you for your birthday. Please accept these flowers as a token of my affection until we can be together. Cousin Bella will explain the need to complete the silver shipment which Alexis—"

Alexis! Courtney's disappointment turned to anger. The woman was trouble. They all knew it. And yet—

Beside herself, Courtney wadded the note into a tight ball. Her anger still not spent, she smoothed it out on her calico skirt and tore it into a million pieces. One part of her said she was behaving like a spoiled child. The other said her behavior was quite grown-up, the first time ever that she had faced a problem and handled it—not perfectly, perhaps, but *like a woman in love*!

The thought was so startling that she was still trembling as she hurried out into the sunshine. Her heart was with Clint, but she followed her feet. And they led her toward the little stream. Maybe pulling off her shoes and dangling her bare feet in the cold water would clear her head.

Donolar was not in his garden. Instead, he knelt milking a cow who was drinking from the stream, pausing now and then to munch a daisy. Another painting for Lance—

But such thinking was cut short. Two figures emerged on foot from the heavy timber and stopped abruptly. They were wearing regular garments, but their faces were painted garishly: chalk-white, slashed with bright red paint. At first Courtney thought they had been wounded, but then she saw the color change to dark blue as it reached the jawline and descended to the open-throated shirts. They wore hats decorated with eagle feathers. And there were feathers in the lance that one of them carried. The other had a quiver slung over his back, but there were no arrows—

But why was she standing here? Donolar was in danger.

"Indians! Donolar, *Indians*!" she screamed.

At that precise moment a massive body appeared from the opposite stretch of woods. How could a 300-pound wanderer of the wilderness manage to walk without a sound? It was a miracle.

And Brother Jim would have agreed. He took one look at the approaching "savages" and roared in a voice that shook the ground around them. "Unless the Lord wills it otherwise, this man and his cow shall make not a move until her load is lightened!"

Her heart in her mouth, Courtney looked up, automatically holding onto her hair. But there was nobody where the painted bodies had stood. There was silence except for the silver-tongued brook, the breeze in the pines, and mile-away scream of a pigeon hawk. Brother Jim stood cross-armed, and Donolar, who had never stopped milking throughout, finished his job. It was deceptively serene.

It was a speechless Courtney who saw the shriveled form of an Indian squaw rise up from among the cattails at one point where the little stream stood still long enough to form a marsh. Toothless, matted black hair nearly covering the weathered face, and obviously frightened out of her wits, the woman ran toward them. There was the look of a hunted animal on her face as she sighted a stump that Donolar used for splitting kindling wood. Picking up the nearby axe, she handed it to the preacher. Then with a little guttural sound that may have been a prayer in her own language, the woman closed her eyes and laid her head on the chopping block.

In that terrible moment, Courtney knew that the pitiful piece of humanity was offering her life. But in exchange for what? The effect was so terrifying that Courtney's brain kindly stepped in, diverting her to the countless ropes of bear claws, the strands of seed pods wound around the brown neck—and something shining in the fading sunlight like gold. Gold! *The locket lost in the robbery.*

Time seemed to speed—and yet to drag. Clouds sped overhead, and the wind swept down from the peaks to say it was evening, but Courtney could not speak. She could only point. And somehow Donolar understood. He set down the pail.

Moving with catlike grace, the boy jerked the axe from Brother Jim's hand. Courtney recovered before Brother Jim.

"No, Donolar! *No!*"

Donolar, his face expressionless, laid the axe down and, without preamble, removed the gold locket from the sinewy neck.

Brother Jim took over. "Rise up, woman, thy sins are forgiven thee!"

Surely the Lord must have translated the words, Courtney thought in amazement, for the old squaw sprang to her feet, clasped her hands together, and, pointing to the sky, jabbered what could only be appreciation. And then she bolted away.

"Would they have killed her?" Courtney whispered.

"Of course," Brother Jim said without hesitation. He was about to say more but was interrupted by Donolar's walking between the two of them and shyly placing the locket in Courtney's hand. "Happy birthday," he whispered.

"Oh, Donolar, you can't know what this means!"

Impulsively she stood on tiptoe and brushed his cheek with a kiss. Then she snapped the beloved locket open, but there was no picture. Somehow she had known. But why did Indians want it?

Both men were talking then. No braves, those—whites dressed for a raid tonight, one that would be blamed on the red men. The squaw? Probably from the reservation out searching for food... ventured into camp...and was unable to resist anything that shone. "Our red brothers can't resist trinkets. Beads and ribbons helped me maintain good relations when I was circuit-riding. Better than firearms—and a lot more holy!" Brother Jim said.

• • •

Doc George came for dinner. His gift to Courtney was a sack of herbal tea. It would build her up, he said—then spent some time on its popularity, local folks thinking it cured everything from blind staggers to poison ivy and maybe even chilblains and dropsy. Of course, a number of his boxes and bottles were labeled "Herbs" when in reality they were legitimate drugs like quinine. Calomel, for "purging the system," was a mite strong, and (rolling his eyes, he beamed and winced) he'd just leave cleansing up to Big Jimbo. That man could purge the multitudes of their sins, substituting sermons for pills!

Courtney had no opportunity to thank the doctor. Mention of the preacher brought Donolar to life. And suddenly they were plunged into a conversation about the events of the afternoon. The meal grew cold as Cousin Bella and Doc George begged for every detail.

"Brave man, Big Jimbo!" Doc George said with

pride in his friend. "Lucky for that four-flushing, jelly-spined pair he fires words in place of bullets or they wouldn't live to tell it. He could drive a nail with a bullet far as he could see it! He's gone to be with Clint. Word has it there could be a raid by white scalawags—understand now why Clint couldn't be here?"

The question was directed at Courtney. She nodded mutely while shame washed over her heart. Unknowingly, Cousin Bella's friend had given her a priceless birthday gift.

The conversation flowed around her, but Courtney heard little of it. Her mind was at the mines with Clint. When he came home—

"Bellevue." The name had passed between Cousin Bella and the doctor. Yes, of course, it was The Brothers who had so clumsily tried to pass themselves off as Indians. Shouldn't she tell them she knew their identity, erasing the need for secrecy? Courtney opened her mouth, then closed it.

Doc George was talking in a low tone, and his usually jovial face was dead-serious. "The time's coming—I would say it's close at hand—when there's got to be a showdown between the men. It could mean bloodshed."

Cousin Bella's brown eyes turned black with anger. "They've no claim just because they're half-brothers—and—there's Donolar's welfare—"

Although her words were whispered, they bounced from wall to wall like a ghostly echo in Courtney's mind. Premonition prickled along Courtney's spine. She dared not meet Arabella Kennedy's eyes. It would seem like eavesdropping—and, in truth, Courtney was afraid of what she would read there.

Troubled, she was only vaguely conscious of Cousin Bella's promise that her birthday gift, like Clint's, was coming later. Everything seemed so unreal. . . even the birthday cake that looked like a chocolate mountain. . . and Mandy's smiling face.

Donolar. Courtney must have said it aloud, for the great, innocent eyes turned to her. "Would you—have harmed—the woman?"

His eyes were tragic. "Me? I cry when a butterfly loses a wing. But you had to have a gift—you must have all that is yours."

CHAPTER 24

Upon My Death

Donolar took Cousin Bella to the "port village" for supplies in midweek. Courtney turned down the invitation to go along, saying she had other things that needed doing. Alone, she would sort through her clothes and spend some more time with the family Bible.

"But maybe we should look for some young ladies your age, Courtney. It must be lonely here for you," Cousin Bella persisted.

"I am not at all lonely," Courtney denied, adding in her heart "except for Clint, and wait until he sees me again!"

Courtney's wardrobe was simple, not at all like Mother and Vanessa's. They found pleasure in clinging chiffons and velvets with necklines that were dangerously near being indiscreet. The colors were those which accentuated their delicately tinted skin and shimmering hair. Their elaborate fans had been a source of intrigue. Vanessa quickly learned the art of holding hers to hide her face momentarily, then look coyly over the top. It was a little trick that never failed to bring beaux near-swooning to her feet. But Mother—well, what *was* the motive behind her mother's behavior? The fans seemed to symbolize it. Without them and with no audience save Courtney, Ana Glamora had a faraway look in her beautiful eyes and was often cross with even the simplest question. "I do not like unpleasant things," she would say, and Courtney was sure that she herself headed the list.

But what a difference when Mother had a fan, which was always when she was going out in the fashionable society which was her lifeblood. Then she became entirely feminine—frail, helpless, her great eyes made violet in their appeal for protection. Courtney paused in raking through her own belongings, trying to remember when it all began. As usual, she felt a wave of sadness that Mother could not love her.

But the pain had lessened. In fact, it was hard to remember what family and friends of her childhood looked like.

Smiling, she opened her trunk, feeling a little ribbon of excitement thread through her heart as she examined the garments inside. Added to those that Mandy had hung for her, she had a suitable and entirely charming wardrobe—not too lavish but not without personality. Clint would see her as grown up now. The governess had overseen her purchases of a balmoral skirt and the crinoline petticoats edged in pink French knots. And, oh, here were her leghorn poke bonnet... beaver hat with streamers... variegated parasol...

pumps. . . and white kid high-button shoes.

Courtney paused when she picked up the one party dress she felt appropriate. The pale primrose color added a blush to her pale cheeks. And the tight bodice and flounced skirt just might add fullness to her figure.

Holding the dress before her, she looked into the long mirror of the dresser. What she saw made her gasp.

"I have changed," she whispered. "I have grown up very, very suddenly."

It was not the dress. It was not her recent birthday. Only one thing could add such sparkle to her eyes, kindling them with green fire. With her dark hair swung up and pinned with one of Donolar's roses. . . *Oh, Clint, I love you!*

Realizing with a start that she had spent too much time with her clothing, Courtney snapped the trunk lid shut. Picking up the enormous Bible, which was almost too heavy to carry with both hands, she deposited it on the bed and began scanning quickly.

She stopped when the name *Desmond* appeared. Thumbing back, she read of how Clint's grandfather had transformed a cluster of potato-sack tents into the first frame buildings. The gambling. . . the cursing. . . the murdering. . . when mines opened. She longed to read more, and would another time. But, as her fingers turned the pages rapidly, Courtney felt a new respect and understanding for those who had come before her.

Kennedy. She read through the family tree. Then, at the very bottom, in a very different script: *Kennedy, Donolar.* Nothing more. Hearing the carriage wheels outside, Courtney was closing the

Book when a bulky, yellowed envelope dropped to the floor. TO BE OPENED ONLY UPON MY DEATH, the printing read. The envelope had been opened—opened and resealed.

CHAPTER 25

A Most Memorable Day

Mandy packed a picnic basket while Courtney dressed—simply but with studied care. The peppermint-striped cotton skirt added another layer of color to her cheeks. Already they were pink with excitement. The ruffled blouse needed an ornament to break the whiteness. But an empty locket on a day like this simply would not do. Cunningly, she swung her hair into a high, loose coil and secured it with a tortoise-shell comb. She knew exactly what Clint would do.

And she was right. "My, my! Don't we look enchanting! A regular little wood nymph. But wood nymphs allow their hair to flow freely—" Clint said as she joined him in the brilliant sunshine.

Clint hesitated while Courtney's heart stood still. It was the first time they had been together for two weeks, and so far he had not given her so much as a "cousinly" kiss when he arrived the night before. Of course, there had been talk, talk, talk. Talk about the raid's having been averted (if indeed one was planned). Talk about sales and shipment. Courtney listened raptly to Clint's accounts to his aunt, loving the deep resonance of his voice but understanding very little of what he said. And then there had been talk of all that had gone on at the Mansion. Courtney had not joined in the conversation, for she understood very little of it—or, rather, the motives behind it all.

Not that she had been bored or felt ignored. It was amazing how she had settled so peacefully into the beautiful surroundings. There were dangers—of that she was sure—but they were a part of her new life and she was a part of this family . . . a part of Clint no matter where life took him.

The picnic was Cousin Bella's not-so-subtle suggestion. And Courtney loved her for it. In fact, she had come to love Arabella Kennedy very much indeed. There was nothing she would not do for her distant cousin who felt so close, and she knew that the feeling was mutual . . .

Now Clint was bending down to remove the comb and slip it into his breast pocket. "Wood nymphs do not have birthdays," he said with a twinkle in his eye, "so it is unnecessary to make any attempt to look older!"

Clint gave a little gasp of admiration as the heavy tresses fell to her waist in a soft black cloud. Taking a step forward, he stopped. The twinkle was gone from his eye. "I like the smooth center part. I like your hair combed sleekly and severely." His voice became husky. "I like your looking like a little girl—*my* little girl—"

A twig snapped. The spell was broken. Courtney wondered if it could be recaptured.

"I'm *not* a little girl. I'm going on 18!" With the

sides of her skirt fanned wide, she did a mock bow.

Clint's laugh was a compliment. "Why, if I didn't know my little Madonna so well, I would say she had mastered the art of flirting," he told two chattering squirrels. Then, to Courtney, "Come on, *you*!"

And, with hands laced together, they strolled through the knee-high daisies and toward a bluff where there was a good view on the river below. It was there that they shared the lunch which Clint said would feed the entire crew at the mines.

"Would that," Courtney began softly as she accepted a chicken leg, "include the Worthington workers?"

Clint frowned, then concentrated on fishing a dill pickle from the jar. "The Kennedy crew has taken care of it all," he said, pulling the cucumber out with a triumphant smile. "It's taking longer than I thought to get Alexis' small share squared away—complications keep arising to detain her."

Courtney did not meet his eyes. "Does she wish to be detained?"

Courtney did not see Clint's look of amusement. "I doubt it. She wants to get on with the annulment—"

Courtney's heart pounded. Surely her shaking was visible. "Then she will be free—as if the marriage had never been?"

Clint's bronze-tipped lashes flickered slightly. "It never was much of a marriage—one of convenience—"

Courtney rose and smoothed her skirt, her eyes brilliant with unshed tears. "Money, you mean!" she said, clenching her fists behind her. "Beauty in exchange for money. It's an old story—one I hoped

I would never hear again."

"And you need not, darling." Clint had risen, and his eyes were flashing in a way she had not seen before. "It has nothing to do with us."

He took one step toward her. She backed away. "It has *everything*. Would *you* marry without love?"

"People are different, Courtney. Values vary, and some do not take marriage as a sacred commitment. Sometimes love comes uninvited. And with a woman like Alexis, it is possible that it can leave by the same door. But with me—"

A nervous sob caught in her throat. "Yes, with you?"

Clint looked into the upturned face almost sternly. Then he groaned. "With me, you *know* it's different. Marriages may not be made in heaven, but they should end up there!"

A little wind, weary of its game in the pine trees, swept down to lift the silk-ebony tendrils of Courtney's hair, wrapping them around his handsome face and, she was convinced, around his heart. For 30 throbbing seconds steel-blue eyes looked deep into the inviting brown ones. Then Clint turned away. Looking into the churling waters below, he said softly, "There is so much we need to talk about, Courtney—"

And, as if in answer, Clint whirled and reached out his arms. Courtney walked into them wordlessly.

When he said nothing, for one tormenting second the flaming-haired beauty with the pouting red mouth and great innocent, green eyes—soon to be freed from her cage of marriage—floated before her eyes. Then Clint pressed his lips against the top of her head and the vision floated away.

"I brought your birthday present," Clint said at length. He fumbled in his pocket and withdrew a dainty silver chain from which hung a cross. "Read the inscription aloud," he said.

Through a mist of tears Courtney read the words: *God is love.* And beneath the Bible quotation were his initials and hers.

"Stop crying," Clint said tenderly, "and on your next birthday I will tell you what the words mean."

"I already know," Courtney sobbed while her heart sang a beautiful love song. She knew. She had always known that Clint was in love with her. "O ye of little faith," she chided herself.

Walking home, everything whispered of love—the needled canopy of the pines above them, the coos of the mourning dove, and the very grass upon which they stepped as they walked hand in hand.

The sun set in a blaze of crimson glory, and, remembering Arabella Kennedy's hard-and-fast rule about the dinner hour, together they laughed—the sound of their laughter echoing against the purpling hills.

Lights in the windows of scattered cabins flickered on. Men were going home to their families. As they topped a little rise, Courtney saw the night-lights at the mines. So different, she thought with an unexplainable shudder, from those in the homes. Those lights shone to protect against danger, while the lighted windows of home were a beacon to safety.

But when the Mansion-in-the-Wild came into view with every window shining with steady brilliancy, the thought went away. In fact, all turmoil in her young life had subsided. Was it possible that she had been here such a short time and that God in His goodness had resolved everything so beautifully—made her troubled life startlingly simple?

With a heartful of love, Courtney smiled at the man she fully intended to marry. She wished things could go on like this most memorable day of her life forever.

She should have known they would not.

CHAPTER 26
The Third Reason

July was unmercifully hot. As much as Courtney disliked electrical storms, she welcomed the rain that resulted on the night of the month's exit. This morning was bright and there was a welcome breeze—so pleasant that nobody could have expected it to be a day that changed Courtney's life.

Courtney was surprised when Cousin Bella failed to make an appearance at breakfast. "Says she's feelin' her age, Miz Courtney," Mandy explained as she skillfully flipped buckwheat cakes onto Courtney's plate.

"That is unlike Cousin Bella, Mandy."

Mandy looked a little troubled. Then a white-toothed smile brightened the dark face. "No cause you-all worryin' none now. Miz Arabella she's gonna be fine—says she can afford takin' life easier now that she's got herself a helper. Left a list for you 'round here somewheres—and when she's feelin' a little more pert-like, Miz Arabella's wantin' to see you."

Courtney studied the list and set to work on sorting the writing she had done for her cousin. As she worked in the library, she was tempted—as she had been several times—to take another look at the ancient envelope she had found hidden away in the family Bible. But, conquering the temptation, she went out into the sunshine. Perhaps Cousin Bella would reveal its contents to her at their meeting later in the day. And, should the conversation take the right turn, Courtney decided she would inquire about the name entered and removed from below Efraim's. Then, she thought with a frown of concentration as she mounted the little mare, the subject of the Bellevue brothers would come up. It seemed a bit strange that here at the Mansion she was made to feel like one of the family in most matters while kept completely in the dark on others.

"You-all remember takin' the eggs to Miz Morley over by the river now. She's doin' poorly after that last baby—and I done baked her a cake," Mandy called from the kitchen.

She would remember, Courtney promised. But first she wanted a bit of a ride around the countryside. And, yes, of course, she would be careful.

"Be careful." Those had been Clint's last words as he left for the new dig beyond the present mines. He wanted her safe and sound when he returned. The very thought of his return quickened her pulse and made it essential to nudge the mare gently, signaling her to ride like the wind. Over the meadows. . .across the countryside. . .her hair floating behind her in a midnight mane. "Thank You for life, Lord! Thank You for love!" her heart sang.

Donolar waved in frantic invitation as Courtney passed. There was a look of pleading on the childlike face, but for the first time Courtney felt compelled to ride on. It was usually a new rose he wanted to share. She waved back and called out that she would stop on her way back.

Courtney delivered the food to the Morleys. Usually she talked with the far-apart neighbors, relaying her cousin's compliments and talking with the shy little flock. Today, however, she cut her visit short. Something about Donolar's wave troubled her. Perhaps she should go back, if only for a moment; then she could take the trail into the darker stretch of woods. She reined in and turned the mare toward Innisfree.

"Is there something wrong, Donolar?" Courtney asked as she dismounted.

It struck her that she had never seen the boy's face so pallid. Donolar nodded, his cap of curls glinting in the sun. "You must not go into the woods today, Courtney—*please*—"

His nostrils had turned faintly green. Courtney was frightened. "All right, Donolar," she humored him, "but is there a special reason?"

"They were here. Now they are there."

"Who, Donolar? Is someone trying to harm you?"

Again the nod. "Murderers. Thieves. Robbers. Him and her. They laughed at me—said Elisha would call the she-bears out to eat me like it was in the Bible—"

Poor Donolar. Poor, sweet child. "No, Donolar, that was a different story. God won't let that happen to you."

"But He let them kill my butterfly!"

Now there was a pitiful sob, and Courtney saw fat tears well up in the expressionless eyes and roll one by one down the smooth cheeks. Comfortingly, she took his hand.

"Can you pull yourself together and tell me about it? None of us will let anybody take advantage of you."

"Oh, but, Courtney, it's not just me and my butterflies. It's Miss Arabella . . . and Clint . . . and *you*. And I can't let them get at you—and you so good to us all—and so special to your cousin—and to Clint. Don't go—*don't*!"

"I promised you, and I never go back on promises, Donolar. You can count on me. But can you tell me just a little about—about *him* and *her*?"

The blue eyes looked blank, as if he had not understood. Then, concentrating, Donolar mumbled, "One of The Brothers . . . and the bad, bad woman. They want me out of the way . . ."

"Yes?" Courtney strained to hear just a few more words. There were none that made sense. Donolar's voice changed. His face became a mask and, rocking back and forth, he began reciting a sonnet unknown to her.

There could be no doubt as to the identity of the "bad man and bad woman." One of the Bellevues, of course—Clint's half-brother—and Alexis. There was little telling what they were plotting. It would be dangerous to discredit Donolar's broken story. Cousin Bella must know at once.

But it was immediately obvious that Arabella Kennedy had other matters on her mind. She was waiting for Courtney in the parlor, sitting stiffly on the horsehair sofa. Courtney waited until Cousin Bella motioned her to a nearby chair and then sat down. There was something formidable about the older woman's behavior—something that made Courtney ill at ease.

"Are you feeling better?" Courtney asked anxiously.

Cousin Bella waved the question away. "Something has happened, Courtney—something which makes it necessary for me to discuss my third reason for wanting you here sooner than I had planned."

Courtney leaned forward. "What happened while I was away—"

"I don't know when it happened—that's the problem. There is a sacred letter in the family Bible—"

"Yes, I saw it."

Cousin Bella took a deep gulp of air. "It has been opened! I know that you would never tamper with something so private, which leads me to believe it has fallen into the wrong hands. It has to do with—time to explain later. For now I must protect my interests, protect us all. And you, my dear—you whom I have come to love as my own—will be called upon to help."

Courtney rose and stood beside her cousin, one hand on the trembling shoulder. "Anything—*anything* you ask!"

There was dead silence. And then, "I want you to become Clint's wife..."

CHAPTER 27
Heartbreak

For a while Courtney stood still, trying to piece together her conversation with Arabella Kennedy. Logs snapped and crackled in the great stone fireplace. Courtney was deaf to the welcoming sound. Deaf, too, to the contented purring-presence of "Mouser," the kitchen tabbycat who, for reasons known only to herself, had decided to bring her two black kittens with their shoe-button eyes upstairs and bed them down on the bearskin rug before the fire. So deceptively homey . . .

Mindlessly, Courtney pulled the cat family safely out of scorching distance. "I won't take you out," she promised Mouser. "It would break your heart—and one broken heart is enough for now—"

It all came back then. Courtney was pacing back and forth waiting for the harsh reality to come when it swept over her like a tidal wave, robbing her of all reason.

Cousin Bella, whom she had loved and trusted,

was of no higher principle than Mother—and the ancestors before!

And Clint. *Oh, dear Lord, no—not Clint*, her young heart cried out.

And then she stopped her prayer. Wasn't she asking the impossible of God—asking that He undo the past? In a conspiracy, both parties had to know. Clint had helped—

In a flash, like a scene on painted canvas, the generations marched before her, always in sinister conflict. Money, stockpiles of money—the Glamora "coal-pickers" looked upon with disdain by the blue-blooded Bellevues. But what a sham—oh, what a sham! Aristocracy could not be cultivated, but it could be bought. Oh, the emptiness of it all—the shallow, glittering emptiness. Courtney had made up her mind long ago that she would live and die a spinster before she would be the medium of exchange in a marriage of convenience. Terms made no difference.

The logs shifted in the grate. Courtney did not bother to put on another one. There was no need for a fire; it was just Mrs. Rueben's idea of drying things out after the summer rain. They had all been so kind—so very kind. Maybe that was part of the trouble, the part she had failed to see coming. Even though she had felt lonely and unloved, there had never been a need for responsibility. Courtney realized now that she had lived the same shallow life here. Her days had been filled with her own pleasures. And what had she done for others? True, she had said there was nothing she would not do for Cousin Bella. But not this. *Not this!*

There always had to be a price. She should have

known her newfound happiness would not last otherwise.

Courtney stopped pacing suddenly. Was there the smallest chance that Clint did *not* know Aunt Bella's matchmaking scheme—had been as blissfully ignorant as she? It was high unlikely. But one thing was certain: Never, never in a million years, would she let the young, handsome, vibrantly alive Clint Desmond be caught up in a web of someone else's making. She loved him with all her heart, but he would never, ever know how deep that love went.

The initial shock that Courtney had felt earlier in the evening had worn off, but the heartbreak remained. Once again her world had split in half. Remembering the fatal conversation, Courtney felt the blood rush to her face and threaten to break through the delicate, ivory skin.

"I suppose you wonder why I have not told you sooner," Cousin Bella had continued without waiting for Courtney's reaction to her announcement that she wished Courtney to become Clint's wife. "I wanted to see your reaction to life here in the new land—and may I say that you have charmed the natives and behaved like a thoroughbred! Too, it seemed wise that you and Clint become acquainted—maybe even fall a little in love. I know you are young yet—my, my, child, I am afraid I have shocked you out of your wits! I warned you that I am highly opinionated and outspoken—no shilly-shallying. But, alas, I fear I have overdone it."

Courtney's dark eyes had clouded with shock and disillusionment. Her breath refused to go beyond the hollow in her pale throat. And her heart beat the tempo of a dirge.

"I—I—I have not even come out—" she said foolishly.

Arabella Kennedy's laugh was a near-cackle. "Oh, Courtney, can you imagine a *debut* here with a stag line of fur-trappers, miners, and young braves?"

Courtney could not. Neither could she imagine that her cousin was suggesting an arranged marriage. *An arrangement*. She shuddered.

"Well, Courtney?"

"I—I—I guess I just don't understand."

Cousin Bella looked at Courtney with the appraising eyes of a stranger. "You are right for each other! But, of course, I couldn't be sure about that until there was a trial period. So, to answer your question —as you know, I am not a young woman—no, don't object like Doc George, who spends more time with my liver than my heart! And there are some matters I must make sure of if the good Lord will let me live long enough—that this house and the mines fall into the right hands, that the needy hereabouts are cared for, and Donolar's welfare—but we will not go into that—"

Cousin Bella went on talking about Clint's being her legal heir and about her affection for Courtney. But Courtney hardly heard. She was thinking of the letter. There could be no doubt that Cousin Bella's discovery that the contents had been tampered with was responsible for her moving ahead of her schedule in the matchmaking. And there was little doubt that the mischief of the Bellevue Brothers and the reappearance of Alexis Worthington Villard played some part in the mysterious puzzle.

"So when can I expect your answer, my dear? If I could have it now—"

"Oh, no!" the words were wrenched from Courtney's bleeding heart. "I mean—you are very kind and—and—" Courtney paused and prayed for the Lord to put the right words in her mouth. And her prayer was answered. "I must consult with Mother—"

Cousin Bella snorted. "Your mother, as we both know, is undoubtedly the toast of London by now!"

"Did—did my mother know?" The words were a whisper.

"Credit me with better sense than that!"

"I know—and I'm sorry." Courtney put her arms around her cousin's neck for the first time. "I love you, but I must think."

And now she had thought. Courtney slid to her knees on the bearskin rug, carefully dodging the still-purring cats. "I must talk to You again, God. Maybe I should go home. Won't You help me decide if I should go home—only it doesn't seem like home anymore. Those I love are here. . .oh, Lord, help me. . ."

CHAPTER 28

Such Thoughts As Language Cannot Tell

Exhausted, Courtney waited until she was sure Cousin Bella was gone before going down to breakfast. Donolar was driving Cousin Bella to the company store, where she would help Tony Bronson take inventory until the weekly mail delivery from Fort Vancouver came.

"She gonna be a spell gettin' them pound cakes delivered. I done baked enough uv 'em t' dam up th' Columbia," Mandy said as she set a mountain of scrambled eggs before Courtney. "Coffee's comin'."

"Thank you, Mandy, but I really do not feel like food this morning. And no coffee, I think—just tea."

Mandy removed the eggs, wagging her head sadly from side to side and mumbling, "I do declare, Miz Courtney, hon, you-all don' eat 'nuff t' make a hummin' bird hum. One day you gonna be caught up in a whirlwind like Elijah."

Courtney smiled wanly. Dear, sweet Mandy. The wonderful soul had no way of knowing she had been caught up already. She could only hope that

God answered her prayer very soon. Only God knew how deeply she loved Clint—loved him the way He intended a woman should love the man she chose to be her lifelong mate, the father of her children. Together, Courtney thought—stirring her tea and momentarily forgetting the barriers between her and Clint—they could watch their grandchildren grow up here as the wilderness was tamed, bringing shifting values. But they would steer the family ship clear of the reefs of evil by maintaining family closeness, traditional values, and a faith that God could pilot them through any storm . . .

A heartbreakingly beautiful whistle cut into her wandering thoughts. Tuneful. Virile. And achingly sweet. Only Clint could whistle like that.

Clint! Courtney dropped her spoon with a clatter. She must escape—run upstairs, anything to avoid him. But something had happened to her body. It refused to do the bidding of her mind. As in a dream, she was unable to move.

"Good morning, sleepyhead! What are you doing —reading your tea leaves?" Clint's voice flooded the room with light.

Even if she could have done so, it would have been unnecessary to look up. She had memorized the rebellious kink of his dark hair . . . the lips that, even puckered into a whistle, were ready to smile . . . the blue, blue eyes . . . and the strength of the chin that so often had rested comfortingly on the center part of her hair when she was in need of a friend. And then Courtney hardened her heart. He should have told her. Maybe they could have worked things out unless—unless they had not told her the truth, the mines were failing and (*oh, dear Lord, no!*) he was marrying her for money! Well, give him credit for one thing: He had played the game well if he knew—and could she believe him if he said he did not? Shame washed over her as she remembered how, starved for love as she was, she had curled up to him like the baby kittens on the bearskin rug. How gentle he had been, how kind, treating her like the shy, insecure young thing she was. Handling her like fragile china. Letting her grow up and—letting her fall in love with him.

Well, she was grown up now! Or was she? Although she was hurt in a way she had never been hurt before, Courtney dared not raise her eyes. One look and she would dissolve—run to him, embrace him, beg him to tell her it was not so.

And then the incredible happened. Clint walked up behind her chair, planted a kiss on top of her bowed head, and laid a rose on either side of her plate. Dewy with innocence, they lay on the white damask cloth waiting for her to interpret the message. The deep red rose from "the bashful lover." And opposite it, the white rose in all its purity. Together they meant "unity of love."

"From Donolar's garden," she murmured.

"The flowers in silence seem to breathe such thoughts as language cannot tell," Clint quoted softly.

"Thomas Moore—" Courtney began, and without warning burst into tears.

Clint's strong hands were on her slender shoulders immediately, pulling her up, drawing her shaking body close. "Courtney—Courtney, little sweetheart, what is it?"

Push him away. She must. Oh, she must. But there was no strength either of body or will.

And so it was that when Arabella Kennedy, laden with household supplies, let herself in through the front door, she found the two people she loved most of all in the world in each other's arms. Clint was still murmuring little phrases of endearment. She should slip on by, of course. And perhaps she would have if one package had not slid to the floor with a clatter that would arouse a victim of sleeping sickness.

"Well!" she exclaimed, totally undisturbed about the interruption. "I am glad you two came to your senses."

What happened next could not have been explained by Courtney herself. With a cry of anguish, she tore herself away, stumbled from the room, and—lifting her skirts—bounded up the stairs two at a time.

In her state of near-hysteria Courtney failed to hear Cousin Bella call to her that she had two letters. There was the sound of disturbed voices below as she closed her door, bolted it, and threw herself across the bed. When Clint knocked, pleaded with her to open the door—once threatening to break it down—she ignored it. At length, all was silent, leaving Courtney to her misery.

CHAPTER 29
The Door Is Closed

Courtney's heartbreak turned to bitterness. She had so loved and trusted Clint and in her girlish heart had believed he cared for her. It was true that he had not declared himself in a formal way, but it would be a sacrilege to have their names carved on a cross, the Christian symbol of life and love everlasting, unless it was his pledge. Or had she jumped to conclusions? It made no difference now, for between them stood the legacy of Arabella Kennedy—tied in some mysterious way to Alexis, the Bellevue Brothers, and perhaps Donolar. Yes, it would simplify things for everybody if she went away.

That was when Courtney remembered the letters. Why, it was days ago—six to be exact, almost time for another delivery—and Courtney had been sleepwalking through those days to the point that such an important thing could be forgotten.

Cousin Bella had made no further mention of her aspirations or the incident between Courtney and

Clint which gave her false hope. How like Cousin Bella—outspoken, then silent after speaking her piece. Courtney was going to miss her, this distant relative to whom she had grown so close.

Leaving her research on one of the tables in the library, Courtney tiptoed down the stairs, hoping not to be detected. Whatever the mail was, she wanted to read it alone. It would be on the table by the umbrella stand in the entrance hall. Cousin Bella was not one to vary routine.

The letters were from Efraim and Lance. Courtney could have shouted like Grandma Fitzgerald when Brother Jim baptized her in the shallows below the church. Instead, she hurried to the stairway. But on the first step she stopped.

Voices came from the little sun room that Cousin Bella used as her private retreat. Seldom did others enter. It caught Courtney off guard to hear Doc George's voice. And what he was saying shocked her more.

"There's no scientific way of mixing oil and water, Miss Arabella Kennedy. Maybe they're not suited to each other. Anyway, you'd never see them wedded unless you take better care—"

"They *are* suited, George Washington. You know it and I know it—"

Courtney could imagine the doctor's full head of white hair fairly bristling. "Leave them be. It's what *they* know that counts. Swallow this!"

There was a gurgle of protest. Then Cousin Bella sputtered, "Don't you see the melancholy in Clint's eyes? He worships the girl. And Courtney, poor darling, with that sad little face—"

"Does Clint know you're ill?" Doc George interrupted.

"No! And one word out of you and you'll be swallowing that snake oil you poured down me!"

"It's no concern of mine, of course, but I have a hunch you're exhausting yourself with the wrong things. The mines—"

"Is there another strike?" Cousin Bella was suddenly alert. "The tunnel was less than 30 feet a week ago."

"Clint's been driving the men, working off his own frustration, I'd be guessing. The men are on the verge of collapse, working like they did 24 hours a day. It paid off, of course, when they discovered the new vein—only thing being—well, you might as well hear it from me. The tunnel ran square into the Villard woman's. What's more, there's a rumble of thunder in the distance, and the storm's getting closer. The Bellevues—"

"They've no claim!"

Mandy dropped a pan in the kitchen, causing the voices to lower. Courtney could hear only fragments. ". . . no time for delay, protect Donolar . . . bound to explode . . . *pray*!"

Courtney entered her room with a heavy heart. Those she loved were suffering, being threatened, perhaps in danger. She longed to help, but in her mind she was a part of the problem—not a part of the solution. And Cousin Bella had asked the impossible.

Without aid of the letter opener, she tore open the envelope containing Efraim's letter. Her hands trembled and her eyes misted over with tears at the salutation of *Dear Little Sister*.

What her brother said would be of utmost importance. Courtney squeezed her eyes together to clear them, then mentally crossed her fingers for luck.

No, a prayer was more in order. Somehow, even then, she must have sensed that all was not well because the prayer she whispered was: "Oh, my heavenly Father, be prepared to hold me up if there is something wrong!"

Wrong? Yes, Efraim's letter was all wrong. Courtney scanned it breathlessly. Then her heart skipped a beat and stopped. She felt her mouth gape open, and her eyes, dry in their sockets, were fixed on Efraim's heavy masculine scrawl. Only it was not words on a rectangular sheet of white linen paper she saw. It was a door. A door closed against her.

> *I hope you are as happy there as you sound, dear Courtney. It will help cushion the blow of our mother's marriage. You probably do not remember Sir John Ambrose, a one-time suitor of Mother's, back when the name Bellevue was synonymous with wealth. Rather a "dashing blade," as they said it in those days. . . reckless, charming, and some said, a fortune-hunter. A nice enough chap, as I recall, but penniless. . . in London now, honeymooning. . . no mention of returning to the continent. . . both sides of the family horrified that no settlement was made before her marriage. . .*

Courtney read on with no feeling. It was as if she were reading someone else's mail. Mother had known all along, Efraim said, but she did not choose to confide in him. Oh, yes, Vanessa had made quite a ripple in British society too, and Mother expected her to be betrothed soon. Meanwhile, it was best that Courtney remain where she was so happy, since—

well. . .Mother wished their home to be sold.

Mother was married. Vanessa was soon to be married. And the house was to be sold. There was no home. It was heartbreak. But why had Mother kept it so secret?

Courtney had promised herself she would go away. But where? She could not stay here, she said. But what choice remained? It was as if a trap were closing in from which there could be no rescue. It was the same old story: another arrangement. Mother had exchanged her husband's fortune for a title of distinction. For the first time Courtney saw her mother as she really was. Stripped of the golden-goddess beauty that Courtney had near-worshiped, she was a shallow, vain woman who neither knew nor cared about love—

But there was a flicker of hope. Efraim was a lawyer. Maybe. . .but in her heart Courtney knew it was of no use.

CHAPTER 30

The Adventure of It All

Twilights were long in the valley. But eventually twilights, like narrow margins of happiness, must end, Courtney thought sadly as she rose stiffly from her chair and dressed hurriedly and with less care than usual. It was the dinner hour, and promptness was second to godliness with Cousin Bella. There was no time to read Lance's letter, but Courtney was in no condition to concentrate. If the Lord would see her through this meal—

And then, like the answer to an unspoken prayer, the advice of her governess came back. "Don't look back, my child—don't ever look back—just look ahead—" Courtney frowned, remembering, though not wanting to, the rest of Mrs. Thorpe's words. Try as she would, there was no way to erase the memory. Look ahead? *To the adventure of it all!*

Only Cousin Bella, Courtney, and Donolar shared the evening meal. Mandy and Mrs. Rueben were preparing food to take to the miners, enough, Cousin Bella said, to overload a freight-wagon train. And the doctor was "looking at the tongues" of the workers—word having it that some of them had inhaled noxious fumes.

"Probably from the tunnel that met up with the Worthington outfit," Cousin Bella sniffed. She then proceeded to tell of the silver strike.

Donolar's face became translucent. His great eyes remained without expression, but the pupils dilated to add spokes of darkness, turning them to oversize agate marbles. He was afraid—so afraid. But there was something else. . .just a fleeting recognition that moved with the speed of an arrow through Courtney's mind. Somewhere. . .somewhere. . . another time. . .another place she had seen that look.

But the moment was gone. When Courtney looked up Cousin Bella was studying her face as she had studied Donolar's. The expression changed when Donolar broke the silence.

"Then *she* will stay—the bad woman will stay. My butterflies will not like that."

"Alexis Villard can do you no harm, Donolar. But, yes, it is likely that this will be just the excuse she's been seeking in order to hang around. The small Worthington share was all but depleted and would have been settled had luck not gone sour—if one can call a strike unlucky!" Arabella Kennedy turned to face Courtney. "Pursuing my nephew will do her no good. She knows that. Maybe that's the problem—the old moth-and-candle stuff—"

Donolar spared Courtney an answer. "But *they* will stay, too—the wicked ones who say I am possessed with a devil—"

"Oh, no, Donolar!" Courtney cried out in dismay. Then, "The Bellevues?" she asked of Cousin Bella.

"Who else! What a wretched lot they are. I wish George Washington believed in bloodletting! It bothers me that the same blood runs through their veins—"

"As mine and Clint's?" Courtney said softly. "Don't give it a thought. We don't."

The *we*, linking Courtney's name to Clint's, was not lost on the older woman. Courtney hated herself for blushing. What a sad situation to be so much in love with a man that a tiny pronoun, a slip of the tongue, could set her heart to pounding and yet to know that there was no future for the two of them.

Again it was Donolar who spoke. "But they—the evil ones—are together. And together they are mighty. My roses will not bloom—"

"Yes, that is unfortunate," Cousin Bella said. "What company people won't keep for the love of money. They are together constantly, so we know that they are conspiring. But," she smiled sweetly at the boy, "your roses will always bloom, Donolar."

Donolar nodded, his curls dropping playfully over the broad, round forehead. "My butterflies will protect us all. Butterflies can be vicious. We are safe. In Innisfree."

CHAPTER 31
An Understanding

Donolar was right: They were safe—at least, at present. But there was a feeling of premonition hanging over Mansion-in-the-Wild. Maybe it was because of the absence of the men. A month had gone by since Courtney had seen Clint. With all her heart she longed to have him hold her while she poured out the story of her newest heartbreak, and have him tell her that everything was all right.

Only that could not be. In fact, she dreaded their next meeting and devoted nightlong prayers for the Lord to guide her as to how she should handle it.

Sometimes she wondered if Clint could be staying clear of her for the same reason. And then she would scold herself, knowing that business kept him away. Doc George had decided that the "lung disease" which afflicted some of the men could be contagious and had suggested that all public meetings be canceled temporarily. That kept Courtney from church—a real blow. She needed to hear Brother Jim. There was something reassuring about his booming voice. And . . . yes . . . she needed to catch just a tiny glimpse of Clint . . .

The illness at the mines plus the doctor's other house calls kept him busy. Courtney could see that her cousin was as restless as she. Neither of them felt like devoting time to Cousin Bella's writing. In fact, Cousin Bella seemed terribly preoccupied. Could her condition be worsening? But when Courtney inquired about the state of her health, she dismissed the matter with a wave of her hand. It occurred to Courtney then that, concerned as Arabella Kennedy was about business matters and the clouds that hung overhead because of the mines, she was also a little lonely.

The time had come to talk about Courtney's predicament. She had all the details since reading Lance's letter.

The letter sounded exactly like her childhood playmate. He responded to her description of the Western woodland as if, were there no miles between them, together—hand in hand like the children they used to be—they would wander through the mysterious Columbia Territory in a platonic forever-after love affair. Once past his dreaming, Lance filled in where Efraim had left off—less personal, but more in detail. It was too bad that Mrs. Glamora—rather, Lady Ambrose—chose to sell Waverly Manor. Why hadn't Courtney objected? The place held so many memories—did she remember the hole in the hedge between the two estates and how they used to crawl through to safety, calling it "crossing the Red Sea"? Well, she had made her exodus to safety "on the other side," but he had yet to make his. When Efraim came West, Lance would come with him. She did know that Efraim was handling the sale of the house? For some reason they were not retaining Mr. Levitt. Already the Manor looked lonely . . . shutters closed against prying eyes . . . Maj, the maid, had married the gardener—a Swede like herself—and Mrs. Thorpe had gone to live with her daughter. Courtney should have something of their childhood haunts, so Lance was capturing the Manor on canvas for her eighteenth birthday . . .

Her eighteenth birthday. That was when Clint had promised to interpret the meaning of the inscription on the silver cross which, in spite of her hurt, she wore hidden beneath her clothes as close to her heart as the chain would allow.

When she folded Lance's letter and tucked it away, Courtney thought: *Lance is still Lance, while I—*

Who was she, and what had she become, anyway? Sometimes Courtney stood before the mirror asking herself the question. It was as if she were two personalities encased in the same body. She was shy, reserved, and insecure. And there was a quiet air of dignity about her (thankfully, not her mother's haughtiness). But, try as she would, Courtney knew that she was incapable of protecting her heart with the shield of ice she had attempted. One look at Clint and it would melt down to reveal what he called her "childish sweetness" but what in actuality was the love she must fight against. A certain little rebellion rose within her—a spirit, probably coming from the Glamora side—that cried out against being used. Oh, why must women be so submissive? Worthy only of serving somebody's needs—and, ultimately, those of men?

It occurred to Courtney then that she was indeed the same person. But three things had happened:

She had grown up; she had fallen in love; and she had exchanged her old heart to the Lord for a new one...

Now that she understood herself better, it was time that she and Cousin Bella came to a better understanding. It had been unfair to behave as she had with her hostess, who surely must find her both ungrateful and ungracious.

Arabella Kennedy read the letter without seeming to bat an eye. Courtney had expected her to show more interest. Instead, she tossed the letter aside as if it were the rag she used for applying castor oil to her rubber plant.

"It would have been nice if your mother had invited us to the wedding. We could have arranged a hoedown at the British Embassy!"

Courtney laughed, something she would have thought impossible only moments before. A warm feeling of gratitude swept over her. The Lord had certainly known what He was about when He led her to share the letter. The hurt was slipping away.

"You knew, didn't you?" Courtney asked.

"Yes—not that it makes a difference. I had asked for you many times since the death of your father, but she refused. It was a matter of convenience—well, she has triumphed again—if that's what one can call marrying an English title with dollar marks for eyeballs!"

Courtney felt that she was closer to the heart of the truth than ever before. "Cousin Bella, please tell me—*please do*—why did she bundle me away?"

Arabella Kennedy's sharp eyes bored into Courtney's. "Most likely because of the money, my child. Your father was a hardworking man of the people, but he was not the dullard that his Lady Ana supposed him to be. I would imagine he took care of his family—unless, of course, his will fell into the hands of shyster lawyers. Even so—"

But there Cousin Bella stopped. It was almost as if she felt she had said two words too many.

"Well," she resumed quickly, "it's an unbeatable combination, isn't it? Money and title. It makes me a little sick. But then, we've always known, you and I. And, Courtney, you know you are welcome to remain here. In fact, I refuse to have it any other way. And neither will Clint!"

Courtney caught her breath. She longed to terminate the conversation, but her feelings must be brought out in the open. "That's another thing, Cousin Bella—I—"

When her voice failed, the older woman said softly, "Please don't say the words, Courtney. Spare me that. Let me hope. I will ask only one thing of you. It is that you give your answer to Clint, not to me. I have always prided myself on being outspoken but straight. Yet I do believe I am becoming a meddlesome old woman in the affairs of the two I love the most."

Both of them were crying. What was Courtney to do but promise?

CHAPTER 32
Interrupted Proposal

Fall was in the air. There had been no rain, but bleak clouds, like warning flags, obscured the morning sunrise the day Clint came home.

Courtney finished a letter to Efraim, assuring him that she was happy, but—taking hints from both Lance and Cousin Bella—asked some leading questions about Waverly Manor. Her letter to Lance was quite different. She wrote as he wrote, using a kind of ingenuous fervency that proved only to themselves that they were children-grown-tall. In her mind's eye she could almost see his wind-tossed black curls as he tore open the envelope before going indoors—and the restlessness in his luminous eyes as he read her descriptions of the scenes he would paint here one day.

But, to her surprise, the prospect of seeing Lance was no longer particularly exciting. He would make good his promise to come Out West one day. But to rescue her? Courtney was no longer sure she wanted to be rescued.

Restlessly, Courtney drifted outdoors. In the yard she picked up a dandelion, blew it, and watched the silky seedpods float toward heaven like little homesick angels. The bleak clouds had disappeared. It was a perfect autumn day, a day for sharing. Her heart ached with the memory of the rides that she and Clint used to take as grain speared the earth with the green of spring, grew tall, flowered, and fulfilled its destiny. The fields around her were stripped bare of their crops now that harvest was past. But the changeless mountains still serrated the sky in purple scallops, forming zigzag shadows below. The valley, like her heart, was bathed in a sort of melancholy.

Except for the little brook! It continued to sing happily over its bed of shining stones on its way to the mighty Columbia. But above its muted notes came the sound of hoofbeats.

Courtney shielded her eyes against the sun and spotted the horse and rider as they emerged from the shadows of the mountain chain. She stood very still, hardly daring to breathe lest she break the spell and she would know it was a trick of the imagination. But it was. . .it *had* to be. . .*Clint*!

She took a step forward and stopped. For a moment she had forgotten the wall between them. Oh, yes, she would keep her promise to Cousin Bella when, and if, the proper time came.

And then all such thinking was swept away. Clint's face was as white as the snow on the tallest peak.

"Oh, Clint, you're ill—*Clint*—"

Caught in a funnel of dust from her flying feet, Courtney was coughing by the time she reached him. And that was none too soon. Clint all but fell from his horse while protesting that it was nothing.

"Don't talk, darling—save your strength—*Cousin Bella. . . Mandy—Mrs. Rueben—get Donolar—oh, hurry!*"

Nothing mattered now. Nothing at all except Clint's well-being. Courtney never remembered the details, but somehow, between the five of them they managed to get Clint inside and into a downstairs bedroom. The rest was a nightmare. One moment Clint was shivering violently. The next he was burning with fever. But what worried Courtney was the cough that seemed to tear his rib cage apart.

In his delirium Clint talked incoherently of ". . . gas poisoning others . . . get them out . . . save them . . . no, no, don't leave me . . ." and he held tightly to Courtney's hand as she tried to bathe his sweating face.

"I won't leave you, not ever," Courtney whispered over and over, only dimly aware of what she was promising. Dimly aware, too, of the others who hovered over her—until Doc George sent them away. Vaguely, she wondered who summoned him, how he knew, and how the others were faring, as he pulled her to her feet.

"Pneumonia," the doctor said without hesitation.

Courtney was in charge immediately. "What's to be done for him, sir?" she asked with surprising calm.

Doc George's bushy brows met in his frown of scrutiny. "Think you're up to this? There are nurses—"

"I am up to it."

"Yes," he said. "Yes, I guess you are. There's a new medication I'm going to leave with you," he went on as he fumbled in his black satchel, "Too new, in fact, for old-timers—could've saved some of the miners—"

"We lost some men?" Cousin Bella moved to his side.

The doctor nodded with a finger to his lips. "Oh, here it is," he said, putting a stack of small packets on the nightstand. "Of course, some of my *homeopathic* medicine's mighty handy. Steep some horseradish root with mustard seed. Force a half-cup down him several times a day. Induce sweating by packing him with cloth-covered hot rocks—then—sure you're up to this?"

"I told you I was!"

The doctor shook his cloud of hair from his eyes and told her not to leave him for a minute. "You can all take turns—"

"I will need no help," Courtney said.

The others followed the doctor out, asking questions in hoarse, concerned whispers. Things were under control, he told them. Big Jimbo had taken over until Clint recovered, hacking away at what appeared to be the leak, barking orders and singing hymns. Yep, seemed to be working. He himself must get back to do for the flesh what his friend was doing for the spirit.

"God go with you, George Washington Lovelace."

That was Arabella Kennedy's voice, and it was choked with emotion. But Courtney did not notice. Clint had gone into a spasm of coughing, and she was holding his head in her arms in order for him to catch his breath.

There would be no more growing up for Courtney Glamora. She was a new person from the moment she took over in Clint's care. Day and night she sat beside him doling out his medication, soothing him with prayers and tender words, and shielding him with her own body when the coughing threatened to take his life away. Doc George came and went, shaking his bushy head in dismay and telling Clint's aunt that he himself could not do as well.

"Why, our little lady's as self-confident and forceful as an army sergeant—even barking out orders at *me*. If she saves him—and she will with the help of the Lord—we're apt to hear wedding bells. They'll both be pleased and proud. I've seen marriages built on less. If healing can come soon—"

It did in one sense. Four weeks can seem but a twinkling or it can seem a lifetime. When the crisis passed, Clint's first words—just a whisper through lips parched with fever—were, "You've been—here—all the—time."

Slippery-elm candies for the hoarseness, Doc George had said. Lard for the dry lips. But Courtney's relief was so great at hearing Clint's voice that she fumbled for the medication and then gave up because she was unable to see it for the tears.

Weakly, Clint reached for her hand—holding her gaze steadily for one wonderful moment. "This—is—where—we left—off—"

Then he drifted into the first natural sleep since his illness began. Still weeping unashamedly, Courtney raced upstairs and down at a dangerous pace calling out the good news to the entire household, ordering chicken soup and a razor. She would shave Clint herself.

What happened within the next few minutes was somewhat like the awakening in "Sleeping Beauty." The 100 years' sleep was over. Everybody flew into action. Where on earth did all these people come from? Neighbors, Cousin Bella explained in her back-to-normal voice, neighbors and friends from the Fort, the city, and all the Company folks. Did Courtney think they would let her keep the lonely vigil alone? Now they were filling the place in swarms—laughing, singing, praying on their feet, all praising God for seeing Clint through.

Donolar came running with an armload of roses, followed by a weeping-laughing Mandy. But Mandy came to a full stop at the kitchen door. Mrs. Rueben was dishing up the chicken soup. And nobody—*nobody*—touched Mr. Clint's food but her. It was a brazen act, which brought on a heated exchange of insults in soft-vowel English and harshly correct German. Tension released, they would end up in each other's arms.

A good sign. All the mumble-grumblings mingled with joyful noises of praise were the norm for this enchanted land. What was the name Clint gave it—Dream Country?

Dream—a nap was what she needed, Courtney thought as she climbed the stairs with leaden feet. She dropped onto her bed exhausted and slept 24 hours.

There was little chance of being alone with Clint during his recovery. They had only one time alone, and it was interrupted by alarming news.

"Come sit close," Clint said that day. "We'll have to talk fast before somebody steals our privacy."

"We'll talk when you're stronger," Courtney said uncertainly. But she sat down in the slipper chair by his bed.

"I want to thank you, my darling," Clint said in a low, intimate tone that spoke of love. "You're wonderful—doing all you did for me—while you yourself were sad—"

Courtney had not expected that. "You know?"

Clint reached out and grasped her hands with

surprising strength. "About your mother's marriage, sale of your former home—everything. I should have been with you. You surely know that we have worked night and day. Then I was too ill to get home for awhile. But let's not waste a moment talking of things that can wait. You must not be sad anymore, little Courtney. Your place is here with me—"

"Clint, *don't*!"

The cry was wrenched from her throat, causing Clint to bolt out of bed on shaky legs and pull Courtney to her feet. Grasping her by the shoulders, he held her at arm's distance. "Tell me what is wrong, Courtney," and, seeing the stubborn jerk of her head to bring her eyes up to meet his, he said threateningly, "You'll tell me what has come between us—or I—I'll shake it out of you!"

"Take your hands off me and get into bed."

"I will do neither! I am *giving* orders now—not taking them." And then his tone changed to the familiar gentleness. "Oh, Courtney, I've hurt you. Forgive me. This is a wretched way to begin a proposal."

A proposal. Clint was proposing. Courtney's heart turned a double handspring. Only this was not the way she had planned it. It was the wrong time, the wrong place. But she had to know.

"Did Cousin Bella tell you of her plans for us?"

His grip tightened and Courtney saw the throb of the vein on his left temple. "Courtney—"

"*Did* she?"

"It's not the way you think. I fell in love with you when I saw the Madonna face through the train window—"

With a sob, Courtney pulled free. "An arrangement!" She sobbed just as there was a knock on the door.

CHAPTER 33
Departure

Courtney wrenched herself free and ran to open the door. She fully expected a member of the household. That would give her the needed opportunity to escape.

What she saw were three Chinese workmen, their mellow-skinned moon faces and almond-shaped eyes (making them look amazingly alike). They wore only bib-overalls, proof that their departure from the mines had been too hurried to allow for changing from soiled work clothes.

The three bowed low to Courtney, and then, in high-pitched, musical voices, began talking nonstop to Clint. What on earth could they be saying? Whatever it was had caused Clint to pale and, even though nothing about him looked alive but his eyes, to reach for his clothing.

Courtney ran back to him. The three messengers had disappeared, but there could be no doubt that their news was taking Clint from his sickbed.

"Clint, no—please don't go," Courtney pleaded,

her voice drenched with fear.

Courtney was unaware that she had grasped the lapels of Clint's robe until he gently removed her hands. It was futile to plead further. Courtney could only look up at him with great, sad eyes, feeling that she owed him an apology but not sure why.

"I must go." Clint's voice was a mixture of determination and disappointment. "There has been a shooting at the mines—"

"The Bellevues." The name of her own kin made her blood curdle. "Are they dangerous?"

"Very, but at least you, Cousin Bella, and Donolar are safer if they are at the mines. There's no way of restoring peace to our valley until we're rid of the clan."

"Our own flesh and blood—" Courtney murmured as she turned once again to the door, this time reluctantly. If anything happened to Clint—

Suddenly she longed to rush madly into his arms and say she would marry him no matter what the conditions. If he needed her money, he could have it.

At the door, Courtney hesitated with her hand on the knob and cast a small, oblique look over her shoulder. What she saw surprised her. Clint's face was a white mask of sternness. It was as if his interrupted proposal had never been.

Downstairs, Courtney sought Cousin Bella, who sat serenely reading her Bible in the sun room. Seeing Courtney, she put a finger between the pages and closed the Book.

"James tells us that faith without works is dead," Cousin Bella said. She nodded her head toward the buckboard in which the three Chinese men waited. "George Washington stopped by to see if you could give him a hand. It seems that you made quite an impression on the doctor."

Arabella Kennedy had apparently given permission to the doctor on Courtney's behalf, and Courtney replied, "I will help in whatever way I can."

Outside there was the sound of voices followed by wagon wheels. From the corner of her eye Courtney saw the three workmen sitting stiffly erect, as if they were nailed to their seats. Clint was shrugging into a leather vest to protect his chest. Thankfully, Courtney saw that his horse was tethered behind the buckboard. At least he did not try to ride.

Maybe Cousin Bella's restraining hand was all that kept Courtney from running after the group that was fast disappearing in a whirlwind of dust. "Whatever happens, my dear, remember, this is your home."

CHAPTER 34
God Is Love

The days would have dragged had Courtney not accompanied Doc George so frequently. First, they bound up the wounds of the gunshot victims (with Courtney praying for strength when she became faint watching the doctor remove bullets from the jagged holes). Then they called at the homes of the men who had fallen ill from the toxic fumes of the mines. Several had pneumonia and were slower in recovering than Clint had been.

On their rides over the pine-needled roads on those blue-gold autumn-turning-winter days, Courtney had a chance to ask about Clint. He was well, well indeed. That is, considering what a strain he was under. Seemed those Bellevue robbers had availed themselves of some kind of secret document. A letter maybe?

The letter! "Somebody tampered with a very personal letter of Cousin Bella's—" Courtney found herself saying, and then she blurted out, "Alexis—she was in the library—"

Doc George uged the horse forward with a cluck of his tongue before answering. "Do you know what's in that letter?" he asked at last.

When Courtney shook her head, he said she really should know. Why? Because it concerned her in a way. In a big way, in fact. But why was he talking when it did not concern him at all—except as it concerned Arabella's health?

Courtney was filled anew with curiosity, but she knew instinctively that it would do no good to press the matter. But she did need to know Cousin Bella's condition.

"Your cousin has her problems, but you know I can't be discussing the case, even with you. Doctor-patient relationship, you know—confidentiality. But," he paused to smooth his white hair where it descended from his old black felt hat, then continued, "all the worrying is doing her liver no good—not to mention her heart."

"What's wrong with her heart?" Courtney asked anxiously.

The doctor glowered at her. "You're a smart girl. You figure it out."

The conversation ended as they had reached a thrown-together shanty which served as a house until the newcomers could build a cabin. About as depressing as a week-long rainstorm, Courtney thought in dismay as she looked at the unnailed boards that served as a roof and the flapping canvas covering the windows. A slat-ribbed horse browsed unsuccessfully in search of grass near a creek which had lost its way in a tangle of cattails and reeds. A red-eyed hound, obviously starved, lay stretched beneath the paling sun. The animal wasted no energy on barking.

"Man out of work and a broken leg. Wife ready to give birth to their fifth. Came here to make a fortune—well, who knows?" Doc George briefed her before they went inside.

Yes, who knew? "Dream Country," Clint called it, and did what he could to make it so. He would see to it that this man was employed. The doctor would charge no fees. Cousin Bella would take care that all mouths were fed. And Courtney would do what she could to make the adults comfortable. Then, while the doctor spent a small margin of time visiting, Courtney would gather the children around her and tell them the story of Jesus. That was always the pattern.

On the way home she said, "I can't thank you enough for letting me help like this. I felt so useless, so unfitted for anything—even life—when I came here."

"Nobody is unfit for God's work, my child, and He will use all the help He can get!"

In her growing faith, Courtney felt a new vitality coursing through her veins. She wanted to reach out and embrace the whole world. Most of all, she felt a great need to share her inner feelings with Clint.

She was delighted when Doc George turned off the main road on one particular day. Courtney knew the road; it was one of three that led to the Kennedy Company Mines. The road twisted and turned to dodge giant conifers in its struggle to reach the yawning, black holes in the mountain, which—not contented with the fortune the ages had amassed below—appeared to be hungry for more.

Somewhere deep in the throat of those gaping mouths was the muted sound of chipping away at the walls and the falling of liberated earth. Although sight of the mines always made Courtney uneasy, she was relieved to know that the men were working. Their troubles must be settled, at least temporarily.

"Does somebody still have to stand guard at night?" she wondered in a whisper.

"Yes, the men take turns. And I understand that Clint's having officers of the law here while he's gone. Has to take the metal by ship this time—the railroads still unsettled since Villard gave up."

Clint would be going with the shipment. Courtney knew now that their trip here had been no accident.

There was the sound of wheels. And suddenly three near-naked bodies, their faces streaked with grime and hair caked by mud, appeared. One held a lantern which illuminated ladders on both sides of the cave—one leading downward and another slanting as if to cross to another room.

One of the men came to the buggy. "Howdy, Miss Courtney, ma'am—Doc," he said, attempting to wipe the grime from his face and stamping mud from his boots. "Sealed off th' gas leak so's there'd be no danger and blasted th' new vein. She's th' best 'un yet—but here come th' boss, 'n he'll tell yuh!"

Clint, holding a dash lantern, came up the ladder. The lantern made an orange halo around his head. Never mind the condition of his face, hands, and clothes! Courtney longed to leap into his arms and say, "I love you."

"What a happy surprise!" Clint said, making no effort to disguise his emotions. "I can't shake hands, Doc, or—" his eyes gave a mischievous twinkle, "*touch* the young lady."

"I could turn my head, my boy," the doctor said.

Clint laughed. He told them about the new strike,

and how it necessitated his engaging a foreman to help Brother Jim oversee in his absence. "It's awkward, my having to leave now, but the other's got to go while there's a ship in port."

Quickly they all briefed each other on the news. There was no mistaking Clint's pride in Courtney's work with the doctor. But (frowning) he wanted them to be careful. There was a temporary lull, but a showdown was inevitable.

Then, all too soon they were saying goodbyes. "Look after our family, Doc. Keep a close eye on Donolar. And when I get back, Courtney? *God is love.*"

Courtney nodded, the tears spilling over.

CHAPTER 35
Reversal

A gloomy Sunday dismissed November. After a mild fall, December came screaming down the Columbia, drenching the farms with rain and filling every tributary to the river with muddy water. The little stream behind Innisfree overflowed, causing Donolar to become even more moody than he had been of late. He wept for his butterflies.

"Your butterflies are safe, Donolar. They will be back by spring," Courtney promised, daring not tell him that their life cycle was finished.

But Donolar was not to be comforted. *They* drove the butterflies away, he said. Did Courtney know that the three of them came all the time to look in his windows, leer, and threaten to take him away, too? But he knew what to do. He drove them all into his dreams.

"A good place for them," Courtney said. But in her mind was a growing uneasiness. What if, by some small chance, the Bellevues and Alexis *were* in the area? She dismissed the idea as foolish. Donolar had a fertile imagination.

Nevertheless, Courtney found herself telling Brother Jim about it that afternoon. It was still deemed dangerous to hold public gatherings, even though the Sunday worship services were sorely missed and sorely needed by all. Brother Jim took to making calls on the valley folk now that there was a capable foreman who could share the responsibility at the Kennedy Mines. He had eclipsed all the Bible-thumping circuit riders and he didn't want them tampering with the hearts of his flock, he said.

It was on the rainy Sunday that the preacher called at the Mansion—just in time for the noon meal. Mandy's cooking was the best natural resource in these parts. Nobody this side of the Mississippi could make sourdough biscuits like this. He held up a sample, slathered on elderberry jam, and did away with it in short order.

Wouldn't Courtney like to come along on his home crusade? Lots of souls could use her nursing skills.

Yes, Courtney would acompany him. Reasonably sure that the rickety old buggy leaked, she wrapped her head in a shawl.

"Will you be all right?" she asked of Cousin Bella.

"What a foolish question! Run along. I'm proud of you."

It occurred to Courtney that Cousin Bella needed her services less and less. There was still that missing link where the name had been erased, but the family history was Cousin Bella's business. She did wonder, however, why her cousin seemed almost relieved each time she left—when one of the reasons for her being here was to be her companion.

To Courtney's total surprise the big, burly boxer-turned-preacher picked her up as if she were a paper doll and swung her into the buggy. "Have to keep my biceps and triceps in shape. Lots of ways we have to battle sin!"

The rippling muscles were an asset in battling the elements too, Courtney learned. Although the road was often a white sheet of water, Brother Jim was undisturbed—even when the wheels groaned and choked. It was like being aboard ship on a choppy sea.

That thought led to thoughts of Clint's voyage. "How long does it take for the trip by water to San Francisco?"

"Good month, there and back. Clint should be home by Christmas. Maybe a lot will be settled by then. Giddyup, Barabbas!"

The order was unnecessary. A lurid flash from the sky, followed by a crash of thunder, sent the horse bolting forward. Surely they would turn back. When they did not and Brother Jim murmured about "neither hail nor sleet nor snow's keeping him from the Lord's work," Courtney plunged into Donolar's account of harassing visitors, as much to get her mind off the fusillade of quarter-size raindrops that pelted the buggy as to seek advice. Would her words be lost in the hissing downpour?

Apparently not. "Those three pusillanimous simpletons with pea-brains would do anything but listen! Clint's tried reasoning, but that's like preaching to some of the bags of conceit I encounter—argue, argue, argue—making me sick. Well, the Lord's a good referee. He'll handle the skeptics. But the numbskulls that torment the boy—well, we'd better move him into the Mansion, I guess."

Matters would have been very different, Courtney was to realize later, if they had followed the big man's advice. But in spite of Cousin Bella's pleas, Donolar refused.

• • •

Three weeks later the rain had not let up. Valley folk who called on Cousin Bella grumbled about wet woodpiles and leaky roofs. There was nothing Arabella Kennedy could do about those problems, but she saw to it that "their bellies are full of the right nutriments." Visitors came empty-handed and went away laden with butter, eggs, a sack of sun-dried fruit, plenty of Mandy's blacktop bread—and something wonderful to anticipate! Since the Church-in-the-Wildwood was not yet to be used for a meeting place, Cousin Bella would host the annual get-together Christmas Day!

The news lighted a candle for Courtney as well. She had learned to live with fear—an essential for women who came from "civilization to wilderness," as her back-home relatives and friends phrased it. And she had learned to treat emotional pain like an open wound. It would heal unless it reopened . . . but unresolved problems disturbed her.

The rain added to her dismal mood. Both the doctor and the preacher had to ride horseback over the slippery roads, and Courtney was unable to accompany them. She prayed without ceasing that this storm had not struck the sea to detain Clint. "I am not trying to strike a bargain, Lord," she would explain in those prayers. "I am promising You that I will give Clint my answer—that I will tell him all my concerns as I have told You . . . about Donolar's babblings . . . Cousin Bella's health . . . the letter . . . and, yes, the erasure . . . even this deep-down feeling

I have that I am being watched. Won't You please tell *him* what to do?"

In the midst of one of her run-on prayers, Courtney had the sudden feeling that someone was coming. "Excuse me, Lord," she whispered, rising from her knees to go to her bedroom window. It framed a dismal outside world—bleak, gray, and wrapped in silence. The rain had erased the shadows, she thought wryly, and made them all into a shroud.

Courtney strained her eyes. Nothing. Then, laying one ear against the cold windowpane, she felt the vibration of hooves. She saw him then. Doc George! The familiar leather pouch slung over his left shoulder tattled that he was bringing the mail.

There was a letter from Efraim. Somehow Courtney had known there would be. But why was she not happy? Because she knew, even before she opened it, that something was wrong.

> *My dear Courtney,* Efraim began (not "Little Sister"). *I find this letter difficult, because I cannot myself believe the contents. I had imagined our mother living out her idyllic fantasy with Sir John. But, alas, that is not the story. It's the same tired plot—their marriage being less an exchange of vows than other commodities which we know so well. Both felt that they had made the supreme sacrifice, given up everything. In short, love died before the honeymoon ended—but not before the man who charmed Mother out of her senses had run through the family fortune, every thin dime . . .*

Mother penniless? The letter fluttered from Courtney's nerveless fingers. All illusions of Ana Glamora's being anything other than a fickle, somewhat pathetic woman who spent more time before her mirror than with her husband or children had faded. But practicality remained.

Determinedly, Courtney picked up Efraim's letter from the floor and read on. For now, Mother was staying in London with Vanessa, who, in the footsteps of their mother, had garnered a Count Something-or-other. Efraim had been unable to locate Mother's attorney, but rumor had it that there had been another will somewhere. Just rumor, mind you—like the strange story that there was another child. Could Courtney imagine his having a twin brother? Unlikely. Still, Efraim was checking out old records and would get around to the cemeteries.

> Efraim's letter ended with: *I don't know how to advise. You are a big girl with a fine mind. Can you manage until I come for you? Then. . .*

Some people swim against a river current; others allow it to carry them along. But she, Courtney mused, was a barge loosed by a storm from its mooring. . .out at sea without purpose or destination. She should have expected this.

And then she struck bottom. That she was without money made no difference to Courtney, but it made all the difference in the world in her future. She could no longer accept charity from Arabella Kennedy. And—the pain in her heart reached downward to twist her middle into the kind of knots that said she was going to be sick—she could not marry Clint. What had she to offer *now*? He may or may not have wanted her money. It made no difference now, she thought bitterly, except that she had nothing to exchange for his pity!

The doctor's voice drifted up to meet Courtney as she descended the stairs. "A wonder, that girl. She's watched me do things that boiled my own juices! But there's more—she gets into the heart of people, like calming that young mother while I cut away the gangrene from the coon-bitten finger of her son. The grandmother had said I'd take the boy to the chopping block—"

He stopped as Courtney entered the dim sun room. One look at her pale face drove him into his poncho and a hasty farewell.

Wordlessly, Courtney dropped Efraim's letter into her cousin's lap. "So Efraim's coming for you?" Cousin Bella said, seemingly taking news of the lost fortune as no news at all. "Let's make no decisions until after Clint gets back. You know you are welcome here. You're *family*—" she paused and tried a different tactic. "Aren't you puzzled about this—er—brother?"

"Somebody's imagination," Courtney murmured, caring about nothing anymore.

CHAPTER 36
The Season of Joy

As December wore on, Courtney surrendered completely to her pain. It was as if hordes of mice had been nibbling at the foundation of her existence since the day of her birth, and now the foundation crumbled. The calendar said Christmas was only days away. Christmas, the season of joy. But she could find no joy in her heart.

On Christmas Eve it snowed. The first flakes were large and feathery, melting before they reached the target of children who tried to make snowballs. Then, when the temperature dropped, the snow decorated every tree and shrub.

"Biggest one we could find," Brother Jim said of the blue spruce tree that he and Doc George dragged by sled to the Mansion. When the tree was erected in the parlor, the two men rolled in the yule log, an enormous thing that looked as if it would burn merrily for the 12 days of Christmas.

The Mansion smelled of spice from Mandy's applesauce cakes and the mouth-watering aroma of

Mrs. Rueben's roasting turkeys and boiling hams.

"It is better that there be no gifts," Cousin Bella said wisely. "We'll have a real old-fashioned Christmas, with a collection plate for contributing to the poor."

The poor. Courtney sighed as she looped red and green roping over the lower branches of the great tree. *The poor includes me.*

At the thought a strange exhilaration emerged from the dark chambers of her mind. Just where the idea came from was a mystery, but it seemed almost good to be rid of bargaining power! The idea would take some getting used to.

Christmas Day dawned cold and crystal clear. Sun, striking the tree trunks, turned their branches to a kaleidoscope of color. The shadows had returned, but they were a different color. Blue. A good omen. Blue shadows. . .blue skies. . .and blue eyes. . .

Clint. Clint, who had eyes like sparkling lakes. Clint, whom she must face when she gave her answer. And somehow she knew that Doc George was right: Clint would be home today.

Recklessly, Courtney removed a deep red woolen dress from the hanger. It made her dark eyes and hair look even darker. She pinned a sprig of holly on her shoulder. And then, as if in final gesture, she pulled the silver chain from beneath her camisole and into full view over the button-down neck of the gown. "Lord, give me courage. . ."

People came by ones, twos. . .tens. . .*hundreds*! Courtney had not realized there were this many people in the entire state.

"Neither rain, nor hail, nor snow. . ." Brother Jim was bellowing in glee. "Come on, all ye faithful! Today we challenge the forces of iniquity, the assassins of character, the drunkards, the harlots—all enemies of the church! We shall overcome!"

"Yes, Lord, yes!" came from what sounded like a thousand-voice choir on the crisp, clean air as the throngs trooped in. Courtney felt a lift of spirit—*if only—*

In all the joyful commotion, it was easy to overlook the one rider who quietly dismounted and entered the side door. Courtney, standing a little aside, was unaware herself until two hands covered her eyes from behind and a low, familiar voice said against her ear, "Merry Christmas, my darling!"

Clint!

Someone poked at the fire, sending a fountain of sparks up the chimney. Courtney, the blood drained from her heart, had no idea that from Clint's vantage point they seemed to catch in her hair, finding new highlights and transform its blue-blackness into a crown of mysterious bronze and gold.

Courtney felt color rise to her cheeks.

Clint's laugh was low and resonant. "Why, the lady's blushing!"

"It's the fire—or the red dress—"

She stopped in confusion. Her heart was pounding wildly and her breathing was uneven. Clint must have seen when she turned around, meeting his star-filled eyes with her own tragic ones.

"We must get away—thresh things out—" he whispered.

The conversation progressed no further. There was a loud announcement of Clint's presence, and they were surrounded by people almost frenzied in their excitement. Was Clint all right? Was there any trouble? Did he sell. . .get the government contract. . .and when would work resume?

"All your questions will be answered in good time," Clint smiled, taking charge in an understated manner as always. "But, friends, this is Christmas! We are here to celebrate the Holy Birth and to have fellowship together. In short, however," he said when the faces showed disappointment, "we did all we set out to do—and more. The new vein is of purest quality, making the mines rich—"

Cheers drowned out his voice. There was weeping mixed with laughter. There were songs and prayers, with some dancing wildly, and everyone pressing forward to reach Clint. Indeed, Courtney feared she would have been trampled had not Clint's protective arms been around her, holding her close . . . breathlessly close. If only the world would stop turning, letting time stand still . . .

The moment was shattered by a shrill whistle followed by a voice like the bellows which the whistler operated. "Ho, ho, HO! Mer-ry Christmas!"

"Ahab—Ahab, th' smithy—bringin'—what *is* them?"

The children bolted out the door, forgetting their manners and pounding on a wide, improvised sled dragged by two mules with bells on their ears. The driver, hardly recognizable now that he was washed clean of soot from his forge, wore a red stocking cap on his round, flat head, and his blue-bead eyes sparkled with a once-in-a-lifetime look.

"Toys, toys for good little girls and boys. Now ain't that jest th' best surprise ever! Best leave th' distributin' to the bossman what brung 'em all the way from the Barb'ry Coast!" Ahab proclaimed proudly.

Then from out of the white forest on the shortcut road another sled glided noiselessly over the untracked snow. Tony, the proprietor of the company store, and his cargo looked even greater than the blacksmith's.

Parents were embarrassed, Courtney saw, as their offspring plunged into the mountain of balls, china dolls, stuffed animals, sleds, and games. But Clint's waving hand of approval set their hearts at rest. And they were as excited as the children to glimpse what, for most of them, were their first "store-bought" toys.

"You will make a wonderful husband and father—"

Courtney did not realize she spoke aloud until Clint answered. "Oh, Courtney, my darling—how I've prayed for those words." Clint's strong fingers seemed to press through the sleeve of her gown, touching the white flesh beneath. Courtney's heart began pounding out the measure of the blood that raced through her veins. Somehow she must put her head over her heart, do the right thing, refuse a rich man's now-empty offer to support her. Oh, Clint would do the honorable thing—keep his marriage vows, once they were made, even if he (*oh, the pain of the thought!*) still cared for Alexis, as some said. It was impossible to imagine him moody, irritable, or out of step with the Lord. That was the problem. She must match that set of values—even with a broken heart.

"—the library—we can have privacy there—" Clint was urging while all but forcing her toward the stairs.

But Courtney was given a reprieve. The crowd had grown silent as Cousin Bella and Doc George lighted the last candle on the towering tree. "We can't leave now," Courtney whispered through dry lips. "Brother Jim's to read the Christmas Story—then there are the carols—and—and—"

In the reverent minutes afterward, Courtney let her hand remain in Clint's and her heart soar to heaven, where she could love without abandon, listening only to the soft whisper of God . . .

She returned to earth, saddened that life could not go on like this forever. The ladies were bustling toward the kitchen while the men engaged in warm conversation. How she admired their simple dignity! The valley folk showed no consciousness of the difference between their shanties and unfinished cabins and the grandeur of Mansion-in-the-Wild—so beautiful in a big, mysterious, and faulty way.

They talked openly and freely with one another. They accepted each neighbor, as Courtney had asked the Lord to accept her when she heard His call—*just as they were.* In the shallow society of her childhood, all eyes had been focused critically in waiting. One little slip—even the garments one wore—could make or break the person. Oh, how she was going to miss these people when the dreadful moment came when she must say goodbye . . .

• • •

As the library door swung open, Courtney entered the shadow-filled room ahead of Clint. There were no lights save the dancing flames of the open fire, and in the minute it took for her to adjust her eyes to the semidarkness, Courtney had the distinct impression of another person's presence.

"What—who—was that?" she whispered.

Clint, closing the doors behind them, had seen nothing. But Courtney was sure there was a flash of flaming hair, and, even in the dim light, white hands—frosty with diamonds—holding something as the figure blended into the shadows draping the side door.

"What you heard was the pounding of my heart," Clint said as he set to work lighting the lamps.

"No," Courtney said slowly, "it was more." And when Clint sat down on a settee near the fire and patted a place close beside him, she shook her head and seated herself in Cousin Bella's cricket rocker. She needed distance between them.

"Clint," Courtney began shakily, her voice gathering strength as she talked, "so many disturbing things have taken place that I feel that I—maybe all of us—stand on the rim of a volcano that is waiting to erupt—"

"You hide it very well," Clint said with a laugh. "Seriously, your work here with Doc George and Brother Jim just proves what I knew already—that you are a true thoroughbred. *Come here!*"

"Hear me out, Clint. I promised the Lord I would bare my heart to you—" Courtney hoped he did not hear the near-sob that caught in her throat. Then, with a supreme effort, she began talking rapidly, not pausing once for breath. Did he know about the change in Donolar? His fears that he was being watched and how his quotations had shifted from the beautiful classics to Edgar Allan Poe? Where *was* Donolar? Neither had seen him today. They must quietly alert Arabella Kennedy . . . but, wait, did Clint know of her condition? He did (a little grimly), which was why she was—well, trying to arrange matters (*oh, Clint, don't!*).

Quickly Courtney told him about the old letter she had found and how somebody had tampered with it. Clint nodded and said he knew of the letter but not its contents—except that it was a near-sacred document which should be in the safe. His aunt, however, felt it was safer to keep the letter in full view of the thieves who would like to steal Donolar's birthright.

"Donolar?" Courtney gasped. "Then that's what the boy's tormentors are looking for? I don't understand."

Something was wrong—terribly wrong here. Courtney felt every vestige of color drain from her face. Her fingers, laced together in her lap, were icy. She dreaded, yet willed, Clint's response as she saw his head jerk up.

"I suppose," he said tiredly, "you've heard rumors—"

"I haven't and would ignore them if I did."

"Yes, I would expect that of you. I do not know the story in its entirety, Courtney. There are those who claim that Donolar is an illegitimate child of—of my aunt's—"

Courtney felt a rise of anger. "I don't believe a word of it! And if it were true, Cousin Bella would make no attempt to hide the fact." Courtney paused before continuing:

"But the Bellevues? They started it, didn't they?"

Clint inhaled deeply. "Yes. They have absolutely no claim on the Kennedy mines, and, having failed legally to establish that, continue to look for something—anything—that will undermine us all. We do have the same mother. No quarrel there. But it was my father, her third husband, who went into mining—making it then Kennedy-Desmond Incorporated—"

"I remember the story—also how Alexis fits into the scheme. But Donolar?"

"Donolar, you, *anybody* remotely connected opens a new avenue. And, if they can't come by it honestly, they'll steal—as you saw on the train—they'll spook, as they are trying to do to the boy and to you—and, darling, they'll *kill*! The weeks ahead will settle everything once and for all. That is why I want you to be careful—"

"And why we must look for Donolar!"

Quickly Courtney rose from the rocker. And just as quickly Clint sprang from the settee. In a single stride he was at her side. "Now it is my turn to talk."

"You didn't let me finish!" Her nerves were as taut as the strings on a violin. And she was unaccountably angry.

To Courtney's complete surprise, Clint caught her by the shoulders and looked steadily into her flashing eyes. She met his gaze defiantly. His voice was grave when he spoke.

"Haven't we carried this cat-and-mouse game far enough? While I don't expect you to lay down arms and surrender—even beg for clemency—"

"*Beg!*" Clint had chosen the worst possible word.

"I will never beg—never! I don't mind being poor—"

"Poor? Courtney, I—"

"Never guessed, did you? I told you a lot had happened since Cousin Bella arranged that we should marry!" Her voice was so bitter that Clint made no attempt to stop her. But to Courtney his silence was a result of her financial report. So, all the more angry, she told the whole story, unaware that she was weeping. Her mother had remarried . . . a fortune hunter who ran through the Glamora coal-mining fortune in almost no time . . . Waverly Manor—*home*—was to be sold . . . everything else auctioned. . What price did Clint think *she* herself might bring? she asked a little wildly.

"Courtney, *Courtney*," Clint whispered, drawing her slight, trembling body to him and resting his chin on her soft, dark hair. "Don't you know it makes no difference? What matters is that I love you with all my heart—want you for my wife and—" his voice grew husky, "the mother of my children."

Courtney wanted to believe him. Oh, how she wanted to believe! The momentary anger, so foreign to her nature, was gone. In her remorse, she felt humiliated and ashamed that she had accused him of being in the class of Sir John Ambrose, who wanted nothing other than Mother's money. How could she have hurt Clint like that? Courtney Glamora, who had been the docile child and now, as a child of God, she should keep her temper, avoid being a—a *shrew*! What, then, held the word back when her heart cried "Yes!"?

Her sad brown eyes, still smarting with the unshed tears of parting, looked up at Clint. "I apologize for my behavior, but I can't marry you."

With a near-fierce strength, Clint held her when she would have pulled away. "Lance?"

"Lance is coming—in the spring—with Efraim," she choked. "But, no—it's more—"

"Money!" Clint groaned, still holding her captive. "It's the filthy money!" Courtney had the confused sense of being held so tight she was unable to breathe as Clint released the grip of one hand. Chucking it beneath her chin, he forced her to meet his steady, now-dominant eyes. "Can't you see that in a very real sense, hurt though you have been all your lonely life, you are following the same pattern—making a golden calf of money?

No, don't interrupt. Would you say 'Yes' if both of us were paupers? I could give the money away, you know!"

"Stop—*please* stop," Courtney sobbed.

"All right, 'I came, I saw, I did *not* conquer.' " His voice was bitter and at the same time sad as he spoke the words with grating emphasis. "Just hold my gaze and tell me you do not love me. That's not too much to ask, is it?"

Clint was right, she thought sadly. She was a product of her upbringing—*fearing* the poverty she had never actually known but had experienced vicariously through her father. The forlorn wives of the miners, scarves around their heads, with an undernourished baby on each hip—screaming in rebellion. It did not occur to her that, grown up, serving them would have brought the same pleasure she had known in service here. Courtney only knew that she could not as yet think of herself as being worthy without some sort of dowry. But tell Clint she did not love him? She would not perjure herself.

A log shifted on the grate. The shadows were lengthening. At last Clint, white-faced and tight-lipped, released her. Without a word, Courtney turned to the door. Clint opened the door as he would for a stranger, and wordlessly they descended the stairs.

There was the scent of evergreens and the sound of goodbyes. Courtney held back the tears, remembering that the shadow of the cross fell across the cradle that first Christmas. . .

CHAPTER 37

To Believe the Unbelievable

The sun dropped behind the mountains, tinting the snow with violet, and the wind was razor-sharp. Courtney watched until Clint's silhouette folded in with the ominous shadows of the mountains. Nobody need tell her that when they met again it would be under far different circumstances.

How right she was that Christmas Day!

At least, her heavy heart said, *be thankful that Donolar is safe*. The boy, afraid of crowds, had missed Courtney and Clint and slunk into the kitchen with Mandy and Mrs. Rueben—hiding in the pantry each time an outsider entered. The two women alerted Arabella Kennedy.

"Is *that* all that's troubling you?" Cousin Bella asked with a question mark in her eyes when Clint asked about Donolar.

"That's all!" Clint said curtly and, refusing the snack offered him, rode away in the direction of the mines.

Cousin Bella asked no questions. Her plan had not

worked—it was as simple as that. Her acceptance of life with all its beauty and its ugliness was an inspiration, but, although she had glowed like the Christmas Star today, Courtney noted the tired lines about her mouth. Dear Cousin Bella.

"There is a carton for you on the back porch, Courtney. It is marked 'PAINTINGS—HANDLE WITH CARE.' Somebody must expect you to stay." Cousin Bella's voice was matter-of-fact.

"I will stay until Efraim comes—if I may," Courtney replied, her mind on the package. Could it be from Lance?

But when the wrappings were stripped away, Courtney found something far more valuable. A treasure she would never have dreamed could become hers: the ancestral lineup-in-oil that used to dominate the richly furnished parlor of Waverly Manor. Cousin Bella was as excited as Courtney. She studied the darkly pensive face of "Big Gabe," then Grandfather Glamora before him. There was approval in her eyes.

"You're like your father, Courtney, while—" Arabella Kenedy's eyes shifted to the portrait of Grandfather Bellevue, "There is a striking resemblance—but I am sure you've noticed."

Courtney sighed. "Yes, Vanessa and Efraim inherited Mother's beauty."

Still studying with pride what was undoubtedly her only legacy, Courtney failed to see the eyes of the older woman studying her closely. She opened her mouth and then closed it. But her narrowed eyes held the expression of one who has reached a difficult decision.

"I'll have Donolar help you hang these tomorrow," she said at length. "When the snow melts, the gentlemen who have engaged your services will resume their demands. They're going to miss you, as is the entire valley, but most of all—well, never mind, let us not get maudlin. However," she went on when the moment of near-sentiment passed, "I have prior claim. Let's finish the task we've begun. And now I am very weary. Good night, my dear."

Courtney stood watching her cousin's retreat. Finish the task? The family history presented no problem. But how does one finish being a companion? A wave of remorse swept over her. "Lord, I'm homesick already," she whispered.

• • •

Donolar helped Courtney hang the pictures. She directed him to arrange them exactly as they were at the Manor. Once again, Grandfather Bellevue blended into the faded wallpaper in spite of his breeding, blue-blood background and one-time wealth. And, in the corner as before and still lost in shadows, hung the massive Grandfather Glamora, whose big head knew no obstacles. If life meant dirtying one's hands—as coal-picking did—fine. And between them hung her father, so dear to Courtney that she saw him as handsome in his clean-souled way.

"Donolar, let's change places with the grandfathers," Courtney said suddenly.

Donolar did not understand, but he obliged willingly. Then, strangely, he paused before the lifelike painting of Grandfather Bellevue. "I know him, don't I?"

Where did his strange ideas come from? Courtney was spared an answer by a ring from Cousin Bella's bell. She called from the foot of the stairs to say that she would like to see Courtney in the library immediately, and would Donolar give Mandy and Mrs. Rueben a hand with the pump? It seemed to have frozen.

Courtney felt a premonitory thrill prickle the length of her spine as she entered the shadowy library. Her apprehension deepened when she saw that the family Bible lay in Cousin Bella's lap and that the mysterious letter was in her hand.

"Before reading this, Courtney, I will suggest that you be prepared to believe the unbelievable."

Courtney accepted the extended letter, already removed from its envelope, and held it gingerly lest the pages—crisp with age—crumble before she could read the message.

"I, Gabriel Glamora—" *Her father!* Courtney's eyes sought Cousin Bella's, but the older woman was studying the newly hung pictures. Courtney resumed her reading, with only fragments penetrating her shock. ". . . bulk of my estate to my beloved wife, Ana . . . with the remainder going to our son, Donolar . . . Arabella Kennedy serving as trusted guardian . . . that she will care for him in his infirmity . . . that all terms remain secret until my death . . . circumstances to be divulged as she deems to be the appropriate time . . ."

"Donolar—my brother—" Courtney whispered.

Numb as she was, it made sense. Maybe, in some far corner of her heart, there had been a sort of knowing. The sunlit bronze of the boyish curls, the almost-translucent skin, and the great, wide-spaced eyes . . . characteristics that, like a gold thread of finest silk, had woven through the Bellevue family for generations.

"The missing brother that Efraim mentioned—it was true. The name—in the Bible—it is Donolar's. . . but why, Father?" Courtney, in her confusion, was a child again, begging for answers as her questioning eyes, so like his, were drawn like a magnet to the tenderness the portrait had captured.

Then she brought nerveless fingers up to cover her face in self-reproach. How could she have let herself become so self-centered that she had put her pride ahead of all else here? *If God would give her another chance—*

Cousin Bella broke into her thoughts. "So, you see, my dear, you *do* have family here—more, I suspect, than you have ever known before. You have a brother here now. You have me—and, if you and Clint can come to your senses—but never mind talking of the next generation! Let's get this one unsnarled. Oh, before I go on, let me remind you of the even greater family of God that you have become a part of. Now dry your eyes and let me proceed," she said in the voice of a lawyer who is reading a will.

"Efraim and Donolar were twins—a story not totally unlike that of Esau, who was deprived of his blessing. What happened brought about the untimely death of your father. But Lady Ana would have no part of Efraim's beautiful twin. To live in a sumptuous mansion and mingle with her kind, those who prided themselves on their snobbish ways, were her goals. One blight on the family was enough—the fact that she had married *beneath* her—but at least Gabe had 'old money'—let me get off this before I become waspish! The sad truth is that Donolar's mother rejected him because of the handicap caused by a birthing problem. The boy would be a burden, she said. Another blight—one which the snobs in her circle were not apt to accept—"

"But he was Efraim's brother—Father's son!"

Cousin Bella sighed. "You must know by now that love was not a part of your mother's makeup. She was bent on putting Donolar away, never letting news of his birth be known, when your father contacted me. There is a lot of money set aside, money that Ana is unable to touch. Neither can the nosy Bellevues or that skirt-on-a-stick Villard woman which, given the brain of a parakeet, they would know. Can you digest all this?"

Yes, she could believe the unbelievable. But, "Does Clint know?" she asked. It seemed important that she find out.

"Nobody knows. Your father made me guardian of more than money. But Donolar is *your* brother. I shall now put the matter in your hands—"

"Oh, I love Donolar dearly! I shall tell the world!"

She ran to Cousin Bella, knelt beside her, and dropped her head into her cousin's lap. And there they wept together.

CHAPTER 38

Disappearance!

Yes, she would announce to the world that she had found the brother she never knew she had—scream it from the mountaintops if they were less slippery to climb! The fair face of Christmas had smiled briefly, then faded behind another snow. The wind had risen, bending the treetops and driving needles of snow into Courtney's face as she, bundled and booted, braced herself against its force and pushed toward Innisfree. Donolar must hear the news first!

The trees stood like statues carved from ice, their lower branches snow-laden. Long, glistening spikes of ice picked up the music which the wind was singing. It was beautiful, but dangerous. Thank goodness, she had only a short distance to travel. She gave no thought to danger until a branch cracked under its burden, sounding much like a hunter's bullet.

Her heart winged its way to her throat, as if—in some strange way—the fallen limb had been nature's warning. Instinctively she shielded her face with her scarf and sought Donolar's cabin with her eyes. The door was open, swinging uncannily to and fro. Courtney rushed through the rose garden, impervious to thorns that tore at her heavy snow jacket, uncaring that her woolen cap was snatched from her head and her long hair whipped wildly about her shoulders. She was only faintly aware of the smarting scratch across her cheek that oozed blood onto her clothing.

Ignoring caution, she ran forward. "Donolar, *Donolar*!" she shouted against the howling wind.

There was no answer as she swung the door open wide. The sound of her voice mingled with the wind to echo hollowly through the disarray that met her eyes. Donolar, whose cabin was always so immaculate! Everything the boy owned had been ransacked, every drawer emptied, every chair upended.

And then she saw the lump on Donolar's bed. A body. Covered with a blanket. A million icy shivers prickled her veins with greater force than the blizzard's frozen needles. Her fears turned to the tangible threat of tragedy.

"Dear God, give me strength to do what I must," Courtney said aloud as she moved forward on frozen limbs. Was it her brother—or was it a decoy? With no thought for her own safety, Courtney jerked the blanket back with frenzied fingers.

And beneath there was a pillow. Donolar had disappeared.

Courtney stared in dumb incredulity. Then, with an inarticulate cry of remorse, she ran back to the Mansion. The circumstances of Donolar were strange—strange and frightening!

CHAPTER 39
Journey to Peril

"You can't make it, Courtney—not even to the nearest neighbor to start a search party." Arabella Kennedy stood rigidly in front of the door as if to block Courtney's exit. "I know how much you care," her voice broke, "But I cannot lose you both—oh, my child, there's no way—"

"I'll make it if I have to crawl."

With a quick embrace, Courtney ran past her agitated cousin to the porch to put on the snowshoes she had found in the stable. Gingerly she tried the snow, then gave a little cry of thanksgiving to find a hard crust of ice beneath the latest snowfall. Almost immediately she was swallowed up by the swirling snow—hidden from the three lovingly-anxious faces pressed against the snow-crusted windowpanes. But Courtney knew that Cousin Bella, Mandy, and Mrs. Rueben would be praying for her safe journey—a journey which could lead to peril.

How long was it before she knew she was lost? Later Courtney was to remember the occasional squirrel, the graceful leap of a startled deer, and then the blood-curdling howl of a timber wolf. Disoriented, she was unable to locate the direction it may have come from. And what had she to protect herself? The first hungry cry became a pack of hundreds. In the long white loneliness of the wind-bent forest, Courtney granted license to her imagination. Out of the shadows they would come . . . their evil yellow eyes no longer searching out the deer . . . she was a closer target. Open-mouthed, with fangs like daggers, they would converge . . . and she would fall . . . fall . . . fall . . . just as she was falling now. She surrendered willingly to the healing darkness.

Courtney's first awareness that the world was still in place was the warm pressure of a man's hand on the nape of her neck. "Swallow this!"

"Doc!" the exclamation came out weakly, incredulously.

"Don't talk, *swallow*!"

Courtney obeyed, coughing as the fiery liquid went down. How had this wonderful Santa-faced doctor found her? And where on earth was she now? Her eyes questioned, seeing the heavy blanket in which she was imprisioned and feeling the welcome warmth of what had to be an inside fire.

"You're at the smithy's, soaking up the warmth of Ahab's forge. I don't understand it. Your survival's a miracle—not a trace of frostbite—take another swallow!"

When Courtney could breathe again, she asked, "How did you find me—and did you know—?"

"Save that strength! Clint wanted me to check on you and Arabella—and, yes, she has told me the whole story. Your brother is probably safe—his kidnapping, a ploy to draw attention from the mines. Incidentally, you were almost here when I found you. Good thing you took the shortcut."

"I didn't know I did," Courtney said meekly.

"Well, the good Lord provides for foolish young things like you," Doc George said with a hint of admiration.

"Let's see if you can sit up in case there's a broken bone I missed." The doctor loosened the blanket.

Courtney pushed herself up on one elbow with surprisingly little effort. "What did you mean—to draw attention from the mines? Has something happened?" Now her concerns turned a new direction. "Clint—is he safe?"

"Details later. Suffice it to say that all hades broke loose at once. It was as if Satan himself decided to set up headquarters at the Kennedy Mines. The Bellevue pair, supposing the place deserted, tunneled through from the other side and, ignoring the NO SMOKING sign, had the Villard woman light a torch—and—"

"And hit the sealed-off area—where the gas was," Courtney whispered in horror. "An explosion—"

Doc George nodded. "There was a crash like some underground giant's protest to invasion of his privacy. The Bellevues are badly mangled and in the hospital at the fort. Officers of the law have a subdued redhead in custody. Fortunately, the explosion alerted people for miles around, and a search is in progress—"

"Clint?" Courtney whispered above the pounding of her heart.

There was strain in the doctor's voice when he spoke. "I must ask you to be brave—Clint was trapped—and—"

Courtney sprang to her feet. *"Oh, dear God, no!"*

she cried out piteously.

Doc George was shaking her gently, calling her name, telling her to listen. Listen? What did he have to tell her if something had happened to Clint? The world was no longer out of focus. It was as crystal clear as if the blinders she had worn all her life had fallen, and she saw, with total desolation, what life would be without him. The fact that she loved him so deeply, so completely, so *desperately* accounted for her anxiousness to please him, her insecurity as to whether he returned that love, and (God forgive her!) her strange desire to hurt him. Now that it was probably too late, Courtney knew that she would have accepted Clint Desmond's proposal under any conditions—and she was not ashamed of that. *Oh, Clint, why didn't you insist—why, WHY?*

"—must go now . . . probably the men have cleared a passageway . . . and I can get through to Clint and the others . . ."

From a million miles away Doc George's voice finally penetrated through the layer of shock in which Courtney was encased. Clint was not dead? Clint might be alive? Oh, she must pray for that. And the little church was the place to go.

The inside of the Church-in-the-Wildwood was filled with cold shadows. Before her eyes could adjust to the dimness after the glare of the snow, Courtney heard a low moan. Seeming to have no will to do otherwise, she inched toward its origin. And there in the corner, bunched beneath a worn saddle blanket, was the trembling form of Donolar! Somehow he had escaped.

"Oh, my darling," she whispered, kneeling beside the babbling boy, "It's all right now. I'm here—Courtney, your sister."

Donolar's eyes filled with wonder. Courtney cradled his childishly beautiful head in her arms. She was still rocking him gently back and forth when silent lines of sober-faced women and children began to fill the church. Brother Jim brought up the rear. His eyes shone with a fierce light.

"Now, Christian brothers and sisters," he sang out once he had positioned himself behind the crude pulpit, the very bulk of him all but chasing the gathering shadows away, "the Devil's up to his old tricks again. He descended upon us like a prairie twister. But we're bound to spit in his face—not by the infallible claim that God's on our side, but that we're on *His*! Now, some of our brothers are trapped in the bowels of the earth and the others have gone to the rescue. So it's up to us to form a prayer-net, one the Devil can't slip through. We'll drive him and his helpers back into oblivion—chew them up and disgorge them two-by-two! Now, pray—not in your secret closets—*here* where the Devil skulks. Pray long, pray loud, pray without ceasing—keep the marathon going. Come on, good sisters, weave the prayer-net!"

The white-faced women around her had never so much as spoken in public, let alone pray, Courtney realized almost immediately. Well, there had to be a first time.

Still holding Donolar, she began praying in a strong, clear voice. She prayed for strength for all of those who waited here . . . for Clint, whom they all loved and needed . . . for the men who were trapped, and for those on the rescue team. She prayed for the doctor . . . for Brother Jim . . . for Cousin Bella in her lonely vigil . . . for Donolar, her blood-brother, whom God had revealed to her.

Courtney knew by the growing volume of *Amens* that the other women would find the courage to address the Lord, tightening the prayer-net she had begun. But there was a strange niggling in her heart—something she had left undone. *Oh, yes—*

"And, Lord, fill our own hearts with enough love to forgive those who have transgressed against us..."

The prayers began, shyly at first, then fervently. Donolar stirred in Courtney's arms. His eyes were clear, and there was something akin to the recognition she had seen when he looked at their Grandfather Bellevue's portrait. Then, softly and sweetly, his lips began to move:

> I will arise and go now, for always, night
> and day,
> I hear lake-water lapping with low sound
> by the shore;
> While I stand on the roadway, or the
> pavements gray,
> I hear it in the deep heart's core...
> *Lord, let it be!*

All night the prayers went on. The only light inside the church was the flickering glow from the lanterns darting like fireflies over the crest of the snow. The storm had subsided and the morning sun was making pink shadows—pictures of the jagged mountaintops when Brother Jim made the discovery.

"Praise God from whom all blessings flow! We've done it! They're coming topside!"

CHAPTER 40
To Be Content

The doctor came first, shielding his eyes against the brightness of the morning. His face was weary, his hands—which held tightly to the battered medical book—were scratched and gleaming with blood. The women stood mutely waiting, their breathing so shallow that their chests seemed hardly moving.

"They're safe!" was all he said.

It was then that the women began to weep, each heading for a husband, father, or son, as exhausted workers brought them to the surface—their wounded bodies wrapped like mummies.

Courtney waited with clenched fists, feeling her nails dig deeply into her palms. The salty taste in her mouth told her that she had bitten into the flesh of her lower lip. Donolar stood silently by her side. At last, when she could stand it no longer she approached Doc George, who was reading aloud from his battered medical book to pacify a frightened woman while trying to clean the sweat and grime from his face.

"Clint—how bad is it?" Courtney whispered.

"See for yourself," he replied with a jerk of his head in the direction of the mine.

And there he was—*walking*. There were ugly bruises across his forehead and cheeks, and his clothes, like her own, were in shreds. But Clint was *alive*—alive and walking.

"By all medical laws Clint Desmond should have been blasted apart, but the Almighty has plans for you two—"

Courtney heard no more. She had sprung forward with a cry of joy and, standing on tiptoe, flung her arms around his neck. "Oh, Clint—*Clint*!" was all she could say because his arms had tightened around her, holding her as if he would never let her out of sight again.

"Careful," he whispered huskily against her wind-tangled hair. "People are watching—now you'll have to marry me."

"That's the whole idea!" Courtney whispered back boldly, then felt herself color. Why, she was shameless!

Even through the heavy mining jacket Courtney could feel Clint's heart beating as wildly as her own. She heard him draw a deep, shuddering breath and knew that what he was about to say was crucial to their future. The wait was agonizing.

"The past, Courtney—can you let go of it?"

Her answer was ready. "I cannot undo the past, but I can live with it. I have learned through Paul's writing 'in whatsoever state I am, therewith to be content'."

"I will make you happy, my darling—and now, my sweet bride-to-be," he said exultantly. "Let's go home!"

CHAPTER 41
The Arrangement

Two weeks flew by on unseen wings. Two wonderful weeks of questions asked and questions answered. Now no secrets remained. Donolar had found a bud on his favorite rosebush and spent hours composing a sonnet entitled "A First Rose for my Sister." Dr. George Washington Lovelace arranged his calls to coincide daily with Arabella Kennedy's dinner-at-six commandment, invariably bringing "Big Jimbo" along. Mandy and Mrs. Rueben, overjoyed with the resumption of an orderly household, outdid themselves. The table fairly groaned with food at the family gatherings.

And now the time had come for Clint to check on the full extent of the damages at the mines, to reorganize, and to get on with the task in which a united family shared. Now that the matter was firmly established, Cousin Bella's health seemed remarkably improved. Clint remarked on the fact.

"Your aunt looks better than *well*," Doc George

said. "She looks lovely. Why, I do believe the lady's blushing."

"Stuff and nonsense, George Washington! You know women my age do not blush. It's the blouse I'm wearing."

Courtney's eyes met Clint's beneath lowered lashes, suppressed smiles winging understanding of each other's thoughts. The grand duchess of Mansion-in-the-Wild wore touches of primrose these days, a small departure from the stark black-and-white attire she had heretofore clung to so tenaciously. And George Washington Lovelace had made note!

A gentle rain fell on the eve of Clint's departure. But by morning the rain had stopped. The scrubbed sky showed like blue lakes in the shapeless spots where the clouds were thinning. Courtney watched the wispy vapors of fog float lightly between the peaks of the mountains and then disappear, dissipating like the concerns which had rocked her life with storms. This was the day—the wonderful day—when she and Clint would name their wedding date!

" 'Oh, let us be married, for long we have tarried,' " Clint had quoted gaily last night.

And Courtney, giddy with happiness, picked up the next line of Lear's nonsensical poem. " 'But what shall we do for a ring?' "

Well, she must not stand here dreaming. Dressing hurriedly in a warm gray woolen dress, with a buttercup-yellow scarf knotted around her throat, a starry-eyed Courtney met an adoring Clint at the foot of the stairs.

Wordlessly they turned toward Innisfree, waving to Donolar as they walked hand in hand toward the little stream. It ran full now, busy with its winter job of watering the always-thirsty Columbia. But, come spring, it would rest and let the wild roses play along its banks. Not spoiling the moment with conversation, they watched the busy stream, rejuvenated by the promising sun, spread out and pick up tempo as—ruffled with foam—it sprinted playfully between two giant rocks and disappeared.

Turning upstream, the two of them hiked up and over the rolling knolls, pointing out the silent splendor of the hills—patched together by occasional scraps of unmelted snow—which led to green-clothed mountains rising higher and higher above the valley floor. How beautiful they were, so tall, so straight, and as yet untouched by the axe of man! *Dream Country, carved out by the providence of God,* Courtney reminded herself. And now she saw it all through Clint's eyes.

At the base of the next slope they halted as if by mutual consent. "When are you going to marry me, Courtney?"

Clint's abrupt question seemed perfectly timed. Courtney was ready for it. "How about my eighteenth birthday?"

"Yes, how about that!" Clint's voice choked with emotion. "It will take me that long to believe it is true."

But Clint did not embrace her. Instead, he reached deep into the pocket of his jacket and pulled out a tiny brocade box which time had aged. "This will answer your question," he said in an emotionally charged voice.

Courtney accepted it, knowing that the box contained something sacred to him. With trembling fingers, she lifted the lid. What she saw brought a choked cry of admiration.

Obviously pleased, Clint lifted the gold ring, set with a single opulent pearl, from the blue sateen-lined box which had been its home since it belonged to his Grandmother Desmond. And, with a surge of something resembling primitive pride, he slipped the treasure onto Courtney's uplifted ring finger. Courtney gasped, but no words came.

It was Clint who spoke. " 'What shall we do for a ring?' Why, use the family heirloom—the ring which symbolized foreverness in my family—"

Clint's voice broke then. He was as speechless as the woman he was going to marry. Gently he took her in his arms and looked down into the little Madonna face that had lost its last vestige of sadness. Their lips met then in a first tender kiss with just the right amount of restraint.

The two were no longer tongue-tied. Their tongues loosed, and there was so much to talk about that twilight had flung a crimson-and-gold scarf about the shoulders of the mountains before Courtney remembered the dinner hour. A loving family would be waiting for the news—which was no news at all. Reluctantly she and Clint turned toward the Mansion, inhaling the rain-washed sweetness of the forest, their hearts recording the meadowlarks' song. There would never be another day quite like this . . .

• • •

Wicks in the lamps may have burned dangerously low in the Mansion before at last they were extinguished that night, so great was the celebration. It would go on for days, maybe a lifetime, a weary but deliriously happy Courtney thought as—somewhere between dreams and reality—she twisted the ring on her finger to make sure it was all true. It was to have been her Christmas present, Clint said a little sheepishly, if he had not let his stubborn pride get in the way. Oh, no, he was right, Courtney insisted, in allowing her to see that it was her own stubborn pride that kept them apart . . . letting her see how much she loved him . . . loved the people here . . and . . . how . . . needed . . . the two of them . . . were . . .

The earth shifted in its orbit, framing a spray of stars in the bedroom window. But Courtney, snuggled deep in her bed, did not see. Behind closed eyes she was looking dreamily for approval from the portraits of her long-warring ancestors . . .

"Well, Glamora, we were foiled this time." Grandfather Bellevue's raspy whisper invaded the dream-shadowed world of Courtney's dreams.

The other man cleared his throat. "Not exactly. There's the mining again. 'Twill make or break 'em, Matey."

"Well," Grandfather Bellevue conceded, "our arrangements before never worked. And out here it could be—just could be—they've less need for blue blood. Red-blooded courage in its stead. Shake on it, my man?"

Between them, Big Gabe smiled tenderly. Arrangements *did* work—sometimes. But who would try convincing either man?

In her sleep, Courtney touched the engraved cross around her neck and gave a contented sigh while the spicy-breathed pines went on whispering their ageless song:

God is love!

MYSTERY/ROMANCE NOVELS

Echoes From the Past, *Bacher*
Mist Over Morro Bay, *Page/Fell*
Secret of the East Wind, *Page/Fell*
Storm Clouds Over Paradise, *Page/Fell*
Beyond the Windswept Sea, *Page/Fell*
The Legacy of Lillian Parker, *Holden*
The Compton Connection, *Holden*
The Caribbean Conspiracy, *Holden*

PIONEER ROMANCE NOVELS

Sweetbriar, *Wilbee*
The Sweetbriar Bride, *Wilbee*
The Tender Summer, *Johnson*

Dear Reader:

We would appreciate hearing from you regarding the June Masters Bacher Pioneer Romance series. It will enable us to continue to give you the best in inspirational romance fiction.

Mail to: Pioneer Romance Editors
Harvest House Publishers, 1075 Arrowsmith, Eugene, OR 97402

1. What most influenced you to purchase **LOVE'S SOFT WHISPER**?
   - ☐ The Christian Story
   - ☐ Cover
   - ☐ Backcover copy
   - ☐ ____________________
   - ☐ Recommendations
   - ☐ Other Bacher Pioneer Romances you've read

2. Where did you purchase **LOVE'S SOFT WHISPER**?
   - ☐ Christian bookstore
   - ☐ General bookstore
   - ☐ Other
   - ☐ Grocery store
   - ☐ Department store

3. Your overall rating of this book:
   ☐ Excellent ☐ Very good ☐ Good ☐ Fair ☐ Poor

4. How many Bacher Pioneer Romances have you read all together?
   (Choose one) ☐ 1-2 ☐ 3-4 ☐ 5-7 ☐ Over 7

5. How likely would you be to purchase other Bacher Pioneer Romances?
   - ☐ Very likely
   - ☐ Somewhat likely
   - ☐ Not very likely
   - ☐ Not at all

6. Please check the box next to your age group.
   - ☐ Under 18
   - ☐ 18-24
   - ☐ 25-34
   - ☐ 35-39
   - ☐ 40-54
   - ☐ Over 55

Name ____

Address ____

City ____________________ State ____________ Zip ____________